He Shouldn't Have Been So Smug.

He should have known that she'd had more cards to play. And she'd played them. Played *him*. And how.

She was the woman he'd spent the most revitalizing, enthralling time of his life with. The woman who'd made him forget exhaustion and every preconception about himself and what he could feel.

She whimpered at his sudden withdrawal. It had only been moments since their lips had met, before he'd learned her real name and plunged from the heights of delight to the depths of disillusion.

So what if she wasn't the woman he'd thought her to be? It should change nothing. His body was reaching critical mass. And she was offering… everything. He should drag her inside, throw her to the ground and take it all. *Then* walk away.

Dear Reader,

Being a romance author has got to be one of the best jobs there is. For in what other job can one experience the rush of falling in love over and over again?

And it happened again in the second installment of THE CASTALDINI CROWN trilogy, where I fell in love with my hero, Prince Durante D'Agostino. Each hero I write is another fantastic specimen of manhood and humanity, but Prince Durante has characteristics that surprised even me as I wrote his story. Contrary to all the über alpha males I've written about, he was so open to the notion of falling in love, so wholehearted about it. He was like that massive source of romanticism and sensuality that had gone unplumbed until he laid eyes on Gabrielle Williamson and it all came pouring out.

I mean, who could resist a hero who wants to savor the torment of not touching the woman who has him on fire until he gets to know more of the "real" her, who serenades her, who actually offers the other cheek, and who eventually gives up everything to atone for the sin of not trusting her, for hurting her?

I was certainly not immune, and I hope no reader will be, either.

I hope Durante and Gabrielle's story gives you as much pleasure as it gave me while writing it.

I would love to hear your thoughts at oliviagates@oliviagates.com.

Also please visit me at www.oliviagates.com.

Thank you for reading.

Olivia Gates

OLIVIA GATES

THE PRODIGAL PRINCE'S SEDUCTION

Silhouette®

Desire

Published by Silhouette Books
America's Publisher of Contemporary Romance

SILHOUETTE BOOKS

PLEASE RECYCLE
THIS PRODUCT IS RECYCLABLE

Recycling programs
for this product may
not exist in your area.

ISBN-13: 978-0-373-76948-3

THE PRODIGAL PRINCE'S SEDUCTION

Visit Silhouette Books at www.eHarlequin.com

Printed in U.S.A.

Books by Olivia Gates

Silhouette Desire

The Desert Lord's Baby #1872
The Desert Lord's Bride #1884
The Desert King #1896
†*The Once and Future Prince* #1942
†*The Prodigal Prince's Seduction* #1984

*Throne of Judar
†The Castaldini Crown

OLIVIA GATES

has always pursued creative passions—painting, singing and many handicrafts. She still does, but only one of her passions grew gratifying enough, consuming enough, to become an ongoing career: writing.

She is most fulfilled when she is creating worlds and conflicts for her characters, then exploring and untangling them bit by bit, sharing her protagonists' every heart-wrenching heartache and hope, their every heart-pounding doubt and trial, until she leads them to an indisputably earned and gloriously satisfying happy ending.

When she's not writing, she is a doctor, a wife to her own alpha male and a mother to one brilliant girl and one demanding Angora cat. Visit Olivia at www.oliviagates.com.

To my husband. To my daughter.
Both of you, my one and only.
More and more, I wouldn't be doing all this without you.
Thank you for being who you are.

One

"I want one hour with you."

Prince Durante D'Agostino froze at the foyer's threshold.

That voice. Coming out of nowhere. So low he shouldn't have heard it over the live jazz music blaring its infectious energy from the ballroom where the charity function was in full swing.

He heard nothing but its softness. As if faders had been hit, boosting it, dousing every other sound. More. As if it had been generated inside his head, a caress of a thought, making all else recede from his awareness. An awareness that bristled with responses so tactile that every hair on his body rose as if he were caught in a field of static electricity.

He frowned. What was all this, over hearing a woman's voice? Over yet another blatant invitation?

A scowl seized his face as he swung around to the offending entity. And everything receded farther. Disappeared. He felt as if his blood stopped in his arteries even as everything else hurtled through him. Heat, sensations. Urges.

Eyes. From the shadows behind the foyer's door, they transfixed him. Pieces of heaven. Staring up at him from a face that was what the offspring of an angel and a siren must look like.

Then the impossible creature spoke again. "One hour. I'll pay one hundred grand for it."

His eyes dragged away from the clear skies of hers to the lips spilling that offer. Dimpled, dewy and flushed as if she'd been sucking on bloodred cherries. They were still again, slightly parted. But he could see them as they'd wrapped around each syllable of her spell, could imagine them nibbling and suckling their way down his body…

He shifted, stunned to feel himself hardening, zero to one hundred in two seconds.

Aroused? Here? From just a look and a few words?

He expanded his chest in an effort to draw in more oxygen, to drive blood to his head instead of his loins. He managed only to suck in her scent—clean, with a tinge of jasmine and a deluge of pheromones. Every cell in his body twitched, revved.

Then she stepped out of the shadows and he forgot any intentions or delusions of subduing his body.

This might not be happening anyway. He might still be in the back of his limo, dreaming this apparition as he dozed off on the way to the charity event he was sponsoring. Thirty-six sleepless hours must have taken their toll on his nervous system. It would explain *her,* the epitome of his every far-fetched fantasy. From hair the shade of fire he'd once seen in a painting and wondered if it truly existed in nature, a waterfall of silk his fingers itched to twist through, to a complexion of such clear olive that it offset the vividness of her hair and the lightness of her eyes, to features sculpted and aligned in such an unusual way that they screamed character and whispered sensuality, to curves and swells in the abundance and the distribution to answer his every specification.

But she was no figment of his overworked mind. She was real.

What was unreal was her effect on him. Women had been throwing themselves at him since he'd turned seventeen, and even then he hadn't operated on hormones. Then had come this woman.

She'd aroused everything in him just by breathing those words, by being near. Now, by just looking at him, she had his imagination flooding with images and sounds and sensations and scents, of drenched silk sheets and hot velvet limbs, of cries rising in the dark along with the aromas of arousal and satisfaction.

Was this it? The overtures of the breakdown Eduardo and Jade claimed he was teetering on? Was this surreal reaction the first crack before a chasm tore his psyche wide open? Not that he cared. If this was a breakdown, maybe it was exactly what he needed.

"I have a check right here." She fumbled inside her evening purse. "Make it out to the charity or cause of your choice."

He watched her supple hands, with those neat, short, unadorned fingernails, found himself imagining grabbing them, sucking each finger until she was begging for his lips and teeth and tongue elsewhere…everywhere.

He took a step toward her, maybe not to translate fantasy into action, but to feel her—any part of her—against him, to confirm that she—and what she evoked in him—was real.

She stumbled back. He surged forward to stop her, only to become trapped in the swarm of people who'd materialized between them.

Maledizione. He hadn't even heard them approach. Now there was nothing but the cacophony of their intrusion, the encroachment of their self-interest.

"Prince Durante! You're finally here!"

"Prince Durante, this way."

"You must come this way first, Prince Durante."

"I have someone who's dying to meet you."

"Me, too, and you'll definitely want to meet him first."

He was suddenly sorry that he'd left his bodyguards outside.

He fought the urge to signal them to disperse the throng who'd so rudely fractured the pristine intensity that had cocooned him with *her.* But they might rush to deal with the situation with inappropriate force. They'd been jumpy ever since Jeremiah Langley had stabbed him a month ago.

Apart from bellowing for everyone to get the hell away from him, he had no recourse but to let them sweep him along, watch her recede as she remained standing where she'd first intercepted him in that evening gown that could have been spun from the hues and radiance of her eyes. The last thing he saw of her before the ballroom doors closed was her arm falling to her side, the check held limply in her hand.

He buzzed his head bodyguard, muttered an order to keep track of her if she left. He couldn't risk losing her.

Only then did he start playing the evening's sponsor, burning to wrap everything up so he could do what he really wanted to do. The first thing in years that he couldn't *wait* to do. Seek her out, give her whatever she wanted and experience that eagerness and exhilaration she'd inspired in him, something he hadn't felt in…ever.

Gabrielle Williamson's eyes clung to one thing among the ebbing wave of people. The man they'd swept along, the one who towered above them all.

So *that* was Prince Durante D'Agostino.

She'd thought she knew what he looked like from endless photos in newspapers and magazines, including her own publications. She'd known nothing. Every photo had downgraded him to the man who deserved every letter of his reputation as the world's most notorious, eligible and panted-after royalty.

In reality he was a…a god.

And she'd approached him—okay, ambushed him more like—with her pathetic offer. A hundred grand felt ridiculous now. But what would an hour with a god rate?

The ballroom door closed, severing the mesmerism of those azure twin stars he had for eyes.

A tremor hit her. A second hit harder. Then a deluge broke out, until she was shaking like a rag in a storm.

What was wrong with her? She was the one who was supposed to surprise him into agreeing to give her that hour. To make a solid pitch *before* he asked questions. Especially about who she was. She'd wanted to eliminate—or at least postpone—the prejudice her name had already elicited from him. She'd wanted a fair hearing.

But seeing him in the flesh, even from the back, had almost blanked her mind. Then he'd turned, and everything had vanished.

She'd forgotten where she was, what she was supposed to say, could only stare at him. She'd moved only when the tractor beam of his will had forced her forward for his inspection. And boy, had he inspected. She'd felt…inspected down to her cellular level.

Then, those people had charged him, saved her from doing that rag-in-the-storm impression in his presence. They'd also taken him away before he'd said yes. And he'd been about to. Or she could have been imagining that, along with his surreal impact on her.

Imagining shimagining. She was a thirty-year-old divorcée who hadn't had fantasies even as a young girl. Being the only child of parents whose marriage had sunk daily into the dark realities of bankruptcy and depression hadn't been conducive to flights of fancy.

That was part of the convoluted journey that had brought her here today, on a mission to save her own company from bankruptcy, while repaying the man who'd supported her family during those desperate years. King Benedetto of Castaldini—Prince Durante's father.

After her father went bankrupt, the king, a friend and former business associate, had convinced him to move his family closer, to Sardinia, so that the king could be of more help. And he had more than helped, had continued to do so after her father's death six years later. He'd supported her and her mother and financed her education until she'd graduated from journalism school.

She'd since insisted on repaying her family's debts with interest. But while she'd needed to settle the financial debt, she'd always cling to the emotional one.

It had been because of that bond, along with what had been solid financial advice at the time, that she'd invested heavily in stocks and assets in Castaldini. It was partly why Le Roi Enterprises, her publishing company, was in trouble now. The kingdom had been hit by a steep recession after the king's stroke six months ago.

His condition had been hushed up until his recovery hadn't conformed to his doctors' optimism. His grim prognosis had leaked out, and Castaldini's stock market had crashed like a meteor.

He'd called her a couple of weeks ago, requesting a video meeting. He'd said he had a solution to all her problems. She remembered that call…

She'd waited for the meeting to start, contemplating how to turn down his offer of more help. It was one thing to settle her father's debts and see to their household upkeep, but another to float a company with multinational subsidiaries. She didn't think he could afford anything of this magnitude now. And she couldn't be so deeply indebted again, even to him. She'd been so driven to repay her family's debt that she'd done something as crazy as marry Ed. But…could she afford to turn down help, when hundreds of people depended on her for their jobs?

Then a stranger came onto the screen. It was several dropped heartbeats before she realized it was the king. The incredibly fit and virile seventy-four-year-old man she'd last seen seven months ago at her mother's funeral had metamorphosed into an emaciated, hundred-year-old version of himself.

Tears surged behind her eyes, at seeing him like that, at the acrid thankfulness that her mother's illness had been quick and merciless so that she hadn't suffered his fate, hadn't lasted long enough to see her beauty almost mummified.

"It's good to see you, *figlia mia*."

The wan rasp that used to be the surest baritone forced a tear to escape her control. She wiped it away, pretending to sweep her hair back. "I-it's good to see you, too, King Benedetto."

His smile was resigned, conciliatory. "No need to tiptoe around me, Gaby. I know that seeing me must be a shock for you. But I had to speak to you face-to-face as I ask you this incalculable favor."

He was asking, not offering, a favor? She didn't see how that could solve her problems, but the very idea of being of service to him infused her with energy and purpose.

"Anything, King Benedetto. Ask me anything."

"You once wanted to approach Durante with a book offer."

She frowned, nodded. She'd asked him how best to approach his elusive son with an offer for a motivational biography, when the enigmatic media-magnet had turned down every offer to publish anything about his life. The king had told her to forget it.

That had been before her mother's death and she'd since forgotten about it, along with every plan she'd had, lacking the drive to pursue anything new that required focus and determination. Her grief was dulling to a pervasive, crippling coldness, and there was nothing and no one to ameliorate it.

She'd made no friends since she'd returned to New York, seemed to have made only enemies. She had colleagues and employees, was on good terms with most, but she hadn't forged a real closeness to any of them. Her uncles and their families lived states or continents away and she'd never been close to them anyway. From the men who hunted her for the fortune they thought she'd inherited and the one she'd acquired, to the disaster of her marriage, to the disappointment of her attempts to wash away its ugliness in other men's arms, to the women who treated her like a succubus who'd drain their men of life, it felt as if she'd lost one bond to the world after another. Her mother's death had cracked the last link. *Why bother?* was the one thought left echoing inside her.

Only the employees who'd lose their jobs and the causes she'd be unable to contribute to if she threw in the towel had kept her going, just enough to keep her head above water.

"I feel responsible for your company's problems."

The king's rasp dragged her back to the moment. She blinked.

"Please, don't, King Benedetto. It's not your fault."

She bit her lip on much more. Her company's decline had started with the discovery of her mother's terminal illness, and its slow death had begun when a part of her had died with her mother, a part she didn't know how to resuscitate, didn't feel like trying. Castaldini's recession had just been the last straw.

But she could see how he'd think that, because she wasn't alone in her decline. Many smaller corporations heavily invested in Castaldinian stock were floundering. Even though the new regent, Prince Leandro D'Agostino, had stepped in and floated the economy, the original hit had been bad. She'd heard that Leandro would work his way down to companies at the level of hers, but doubted her company could last until he did. And then, even with his power and financial clout, as regent only, he didn't promise the market the long-term stability a king would. Advisors had urged her not to await rescue, said Leando might even let lesser interests go under to stabilize the big picture.

The king went on. "Durante could revive your company, either with a bestseller or in other ways if he so wished."

That was what her advisors had said. That only a guaranteed bestseller or a merger with any major player would buoy her company. Prince Durante would have answered both criteria. But previously, the king had said Durante wasn't an option. Which meant... "So he'd be amenable to an offer now?"

"I'm not saying he would be."

That stymied her. "Then what has changed?"

"Your situation. And mine."

She didn't understand what her situation had to do with his, only that he thought a positive result might be obtained now. She should jump at the opening. Yet she wanted to do nothing but say goodbye and sit staring into space. It seemed that her lethargy wasn't about to let her challenge-tackling abilities escape its somnolent grip. She sighed. "I'll give it some more thought—"

"I'm *asking* you to do it, Gaby." The king interrupted her. "And I don't just want you to sign a contract with him. I want you to insist on being his editor or ghostwriter or however you get such books written. I want you to work as closely as possible with him so that you can convince him to come back to Castaldini." Gabrielle adjusted the screen, as if that would help his words make sense. He elaborated, ending her confusion. "He left five years ago, saying he'll never return as long as I live. And he's kept his promise. He didn't even call when I had my stroke."

Something trickled through the clotted mass of indifference inside her. Emotions. Surprise, indignation…anger.

What kind of monster would do that to his father, and a great man like King Benedetto, too? And to think Durante had been the one she'd admired most among all Castaldinian princes, his self-made success intriguing her far more because it didn't have the crown as its goal. As the king's son, Durante was the one prince who was ineligible for the crown. And then, *success* didn't describe what he'd achieved. He'd become one of the world's richest, most powerful men, starting with investment banking, then branching into just about everything, garnering a worldwide reputation for being unstoppable, as well as inaccessible. But it was one thing to reject intimacy as evidenced by his misanthrope/heartbreaker reputation, another to reject the man who was his father and king.

"Why all this…antipathy?" she asked.

"Durante blames me for terrible things, things I haven't been able to prove I wasn't responsible for." Okay. So it was more complicated than she could imagine. She really couldn't form an opinion here. She shouldn't. It had nothing to do with her. And she wanted it to stay that way. "But it doesn't matter what he believes. He must come back, Gaby. It's not only that I need my son—Castaldini needs his power and influence."

Scratch the no-opinion status. No matter Durante's reasons, he was a callous creep if he not only didn't care about his father's incapacitation but also about Castaldini's troubles. And *she* was supposed to make him care?

She asked that, and the king nodded. "I know you can. You'll come in with a fresh slate and views, with legitimate business offers and concerns. But give me your word that you'll never tell him of our connection. That would make him send you straight to hell. And none of us can afford that. The situation is grave, and I must be clear. I want you to do *anything* to make him come back."

His words had echoed long after their goodbyes. What he'd meant by *anything* was so glaringly clear, it was blinding. Seduction.

She was resigned to her femme fatale reputation. But it hurt that even the king thought seduction was one of her weapons, her only one, even. Still, she excused him. He was old and sick and desperate to resolve his problems, to secure his kingdom's future.

And then, what he'd proposed *was* a worthy cause. If she succeeded—seduction certainly *not* on the menu of maneuvers she'd use—everyone would come out a winner. The king would have his son back—a reconciliation that was bound to make said son happier, too—Castaldini would get a heavy-hitter to help its regent pull its fat out of the fire, and she'd stabilize her company.

But the damned prince hadn't even acknowledged her messages. She could think of only one reason. His initial background check on anyone who approached him must have accessed the usual slander. Seemed he'd thought such unsubstantiated filth enough to condemn her.

Furious, she'd called in a favor with one of his insiders and gotten his schedule for the next week. Besides being impossible to get hold of, he was also known for badgering the privileged into doing more for the world. This function was one of his traps where he wrung what he could get out of them for his favorite causes. She'd intended to intercept him, make him an offer he couldn't refuse. At least, that had been the plan.

So far, all she'd done was stammer three sentences and got nothing out of him but that disconcerting stare.

She needed results, but she had to restart her own volition first. Or at least the autopilot that had steered her for months now.

One or the other must have kicked in, because she moved at last.

She leaned on the door as she opened it. The exuberance of jazz and the forced gaiety in the overcrowded ballroom slammed into her. But what almost knocked her off her feet was the power of his gaze. He'd been watching for her, as if certain she'd follow him.

Not that she could. Those people who had the same idea as her—of ambushing him here—left her no chink to get through.

He left her no air to breathe as his gaze drilled into her across the ballroom. She began to think it might not be a bad thing after all if she didn't get a chance to talk to him alone.

She was a seasoned businesswoman who'd been through a battlefield of a marriage and divorce, who'd before and since been pursued by men, had thought she'd seen and tried all kinds, to her crushing dissatisfaction. But Prince D'Agostino fell far outside what she'd thought to be her inclusive experience. To lump him under "man" with those she'd had experience with was as accurate as lumping a top-of-the-food-chain predator with a jellyfish. Something very sure of itself told her she shouldn't get closer. For any reason.

She should leave. Now.

She had to pry her gaze—her will—from his first.

Somehow she did, was at the door when a rough velvet whisper hit her between the shoulder blades. "Don't run off yet."

Logic said that omnidirectional/internal sound effect was the surround system's doing. But there was no logic here. There was only the influence the voice exercised, the reactions it ignited. The certainty that it was talking to her.

She swayed around, found him on the dais in front of the mic, his gaze still cast on her like a stasis field.

"Ladies and gentlemen," he said. "Thank you for paying the ten-grand admission fee. But because you're getting…restless, I'll fast-forward to prying some *real* contributions out of you. You have the auction list, but in light of a certain…development, I have made some changes. Now the first item on auction is… myself."

Two

If Prince Durante D'Agostino had announced he was Superman and launched into the air to circle overhead, there wouldn't have been a more drastic reaction to his announcement.

Not that it would have shocked her. He did look like some superhuman being as he dominated the scene just by standing there, the rugged nobleness of his features and his leonine forehead accentuated by the swept-back mane of raven satin, the jacket of his sculpted designer charcoal suit casually pushed back by the hand resting on his hip, his white shirt stretching across his torso, detailing the daunting power beneath. He looked like a modern god swathed in the trappings of the times that equalized other men but that didn't begin to contain the influence he exuded, to disguise his in-his-own-league nature.

His gaze panned the ballroom yet somehow managed not to release hers. That alone kept her heart practically dropping to the polished Carrara marble floor. But what restarted her tremors was what she saw in those eyes—an intensity untouched by the cynical amusement with which he watched the mayhem he'd kicked up.

"Before you get too excited," he finally said. "I'm not auctioning off all of me, just my ear. Considering how in demand it is, with so many of you attempting to talk it off, I'm offering one hour of its exclusive use." His lips tugged into what had to be the most arrhythmia-inducing weapon ever deployed on susceptible females. And it had her in its crosshairs. "I already have an opening bid. One hundred grand."

Now she knew how *mamma mia* had been coined. It had to have been a woman who'd first exclaimed it, as a brutally gorgeous male plucked her strings.

And she did feel like a marionette, compelled to obey his every tug, any reluctance or misgiving evaporating in the excitement his mischief sent through her. She walked back under the pull of his challenge.

When she stopped at the fringe of the bidding crowd, he put his lips to the mic, implanted hot, wild images and sensations straight inside her, pitched his voice an octave lower. "Do I hear one hundred ten?"

Over three-dozen people, mostly women, raised their hands. She'd beaten them all in speed of response.

His lips spread in satisfaction, his pose grew more languid, a conqueror certain of his victory, indulgent in his triumph. "Thank you. Do I hear one hundred twenty?"

Her hand was up in the air before she could will it to be there. Seemed he'd jumpstarted her competitiveness. More. He'd sparked the first sign of life in her since she'd witnessed her mother's being extinguished.

He kept raising the bid, and her competition dwindled. Soon suspense was fast reaching the point of overload.

When a dozen hands still shot up in the air when he reached the four hundred fifty grand mark, her stamina snapped and recoiled like an overextended string.

She blurted out, "I bid one million."

A hush fell. Everyone turned to gape at her.

He straightened, his eyes losing all lightness, singeing hers through the charge that filled the space between them. "Now that's a nice round figure. Anyone willing to top that? No? Fine, then. I have one million from the lady in blue. Going once, going twice—"

"I bid *ten* million."

Durante saw shock seize his mystery woman's face before he registered the words that had caused it. Only then did he drag his eyes and senses from her and search out the new speaker.

His every muscle tensed. How had *he* gotten past security? How had Durante not noticed him before?

His security had messed up. As for him, all his faculties had been converged on *her,* everything else skimming his consciousness without leaving an imprint.

And there was the now-gaunt, wild-eyed Jeremiah Langley. Staring at him like a drowning man would at a lifeboat. A month ago he'd looked at Durante as if at his own killer, before attempting to stab him. Durante couldn't imagine how Langley had ended up blaming him—and not the investments he'd made against his advice—for his bankruptcy, but he'd hushed everything up, not wishing to add criminal charges to the distraught man's troubles. He'd also postponed announcing Langley's bankruptcy until he sold shares that would leave the man with minimal debt. But he'd made it clear to Langley, and to his security—he didn't want to see the man again. Not in this lifetime.

No one knew how things stood between them, or that Jeremiah didn't have the ten million he'd bid for Durante's leniency. He couldn't call Langley on it without outing him. Langley had cornered him into accepting his so-called bid as the winning one.

And *that* was his worst crime.

She had already accepted defeat. This time, she *was* walking away. He might not have more of her. Not tonight. Unacceptable.

He would have more of her. And if he had his way, as he always did, he would have all of her.

Gabrielle felt all animation drain from her system.

The moment her bid had burst from her incontinent mouth, she'd launched into feverish calculations to determine how she could part with that much cash in one lump sum in her current situation. Then that ten-million-dollar sledgehammer had fallen, pulverizing both worry and hope.

So that was it. She'd bid and lost. And he was no longer looking at her. Ten million dollars would distract even him.

So what was that tightening behind her ribs? Disappointment?

How stupid was that? This scheme wouldn't have worked anyway. She didn't know how she or King Benedetto could have thought it might. All her moronic endeavor would achieve was to give the scandal sheets fuel for the coming decade. She had to leave before the paparazzi he'd banned from the event got wind of this and ambushed her. *Leave. Now. And don't look back.*

She managed that, but still felt as if she were wading through quicksand. His gaze had latched on to her again, robbed her of dominion over her own body. Desperation to get away kicked in.

In minutes she was in the parking lot, running to her car.

She remote-opened her door, was reaching for its handle when a boom cracked the silence of the night.

"Stay."

She dropped her keys. Her purse. Probably a few months' to a couple of years' life expectancy, too.

She slumped against the warm metal and glass as if pressed there by the presence closing in on her. She heard nothing but the blood thundering in her head. The presence expanded at her back, pinning her to her support, squeezing her heart.

She fumbled for the door handle. She'd managed to open the door when that voice hit her again, a quiet rumble this time.

"Stay."

She clenched her eyes shut, pitched forward, her nerveless weight closing the door with a muffled thud. That one word.

An invocation. Deeper and darker than the moonless night.

She turned around, leaning on the car. And there he was.

The good news was that he kept a dozen feet between them. The bad news was that it made no difference. And why should it? He'd been dozens of feet away in that ballroom and had still overwhelmed her.

"Stay?" Where was her voice? She'd addressed him before in a breathless whisper. This time it was a husky rasp. Both were nothing like her usual crisp tones. "What am I? Your poodle? What's next? Roll over? Beg…?" She winced, stopped. Where were her brakes?

"How about 'stop,'" he drawled. "Before you inflame my already-raging imagination beyond control."

His voice wasn't the same as what had flowed from the sound system earlier. It was so much more layered and modulated and hard-hitting, the prominent r's of his accent far more intoxicating. Hearing it without distortion delayed her comprehension of his words. Then it hit her and she almost went up in a puff of mortification.

She couldn't *believe* she'd said something so provocative, just begging for misinterpretation. He'd never believe she hadn't meant anything beyond sarcasm.

But wonder of wonders, his eyes weren't stained with that knowing derision she was used to from men. His emitted only pure excitement. "Would 'stop' be less open to unfavorable interpretation? How about 'don't leave'?"

His voice sluiced another rush of heat over her. She quivered. "Still orders, both of them."

He tilted his head. Light ignited the azure depths of his eyes and carved dimples in his sculpted cheeks. "At least they don't have canine connotations, if my idiomatic English serves."

And she did something she'd thought was beyond her, now and forever. She giggled. *Giggled.*

His eyes widened as if she'd electrified him. He retaliated with something far more debilitating than electricity. He chuckled.

She struggled not to melt into the ground. "You're pleading less-than-perfect English skills to explain the inappropriateness of barking 'stay' at me across the parking lot like that?"

"Barking? Still going with the dog motif, eh?"

"You did bark," she mumbled in embarrassment. "You frightened me out of my skin. I think it's still pooled on the ground."

His eyes swept down her body, until she felt it was her dress that lay at her feet. "From where I'm standing, your skin is still enveloping you like a glove and, propriety notwithstanding, you can see what the sight does to me."

More heat splashed through her as she fixed her gaze on his so it wouldn't stray to "see" anything. "See? Perfect English skills."

"I'm sure my English tutor would love to hear that the ulcer he swore I gave him has ultimately been validated."

"You gave your teacher hell? You're pulling my leg."

"Again, do watch what you say to me, or I might succumb and tell you exactly how and where I want to pull both your legs."

Images slammed into her. Vivid, tangible. Those large, perfectly formed hands dragging her by the thighs, opening her around his bulk as he bore down on her…

"I've changed my verdict," she choked. "Your English skills are not perfect. They're horrible. Evil. *Sietto un uomo cattivo.*"

Suddenly the sounds of the night were amplified in the stillness that echoed between them. Whoever had said one could drown in another's eyes must have been describing Prince Durante's endless azure seas and the submersion of their focus.

Just as she felt her lungs using up the last tendril of oxygen, he exhaled. *"Mia bella misteriosa…parlate italiano?"*

She realized she'd said he was a wicked man in Italian. It had once come to her as unconsciously as English did. She used to talk and think in an inextricable mix, a habit that had faded since she'd returned to the States. This was the first time in many years that she'd reverted to the second-nature practice. It felt as if a missing part of her had clicked back into place.

Then more registered. He'd called her his mysterious beauty, asked if she spoke Italian.

"I lived in Sardinia and Italy from age five until I returned to the States to enter college at seventeen."

These revelations were way beyond the simple *yes* his question warranted. But he made her want to do unknown things. Flirt, tease. Confide. It had to be the premium royal testosterone overexposure.

After a long moment when he looked at her as if at a gem with a thousand facets, he breathed, "*Dio Santo,* what are you?"

"What…? Uh, yeah, I haven't exactly introduced myself yet."

"No, you haven't. Exactly or otherwise."

"Umm…yeah, there's sort of a reason I haven't. You see, I'm—"

"You are *mia bella misteriosa,* who's done what no woman has ever done—offered money to spend time with me."

"Now *that* I find impossible to believe. I bet women offer anything and everything for time with you. I bet most wouldn't mind if it wasn't even one-on-one."

"You think so? Because of who I am?" Her gaze wavered with uncertainty. He elaborated. "Rich and royal?"

Her laugh morphed into a snort that would have made a sailor proud. "Are you kidding? Or are you fishing? Women would throw themselves at you if you were a penniless nobody."

His eyes flared. "Coming from anybody else, I'd think that a worthless exaggeration, but from you, I know it's how you see me. For it's how I see you, too. As for the one-on-one basis, that is the only way I would accept to have time with you."

A moan of stimulation stumbled over her croak of embarrassment.

Hell, the man was reducing her to a pubescent state. But he was doing something even worse.

He was obliterating the distance between them.

Mesmerized, she took in the control and power that permeated his every move, the breadth of shoulders and chest that owed nothing to padding, the sparseness of waist and hips, the hardness of thighs rippling beneath exquisite fabric as he prowled toward her, a majestic creature by birthright and by merit. Now *this* was a man to make her revise her stance on swearing off men forever, a pledge she'd made happily years ago.

Which was a crazy thing to think.

Crazier would be to act on such insanity.

She stood there waiting for him to reach her with the same fatalism she'd watch a collision in progress, could think only that no man had ever looked at her like this. As if she was something incredibly unexpected, and unexpectedly incredible. The wonder in his eyes drowned out the urgent voices that yelled that his damage potential would far surpass the devastation caused by any such collision.

Every step closer to his mystery woman solidified into fact what Durante had sensed from the first moment he saw her.

This was new. Surprising and stimulating. When he'd been certain nothing and no one would ever surprise or stimulate him. She did both, and far more, with every breath.

Her effect on him was so unprecedented that he'd done the unprecedented. He'd delegated running the rest of the charity function to his deputy. And he'd sent his bodyguards away, forbade them to follow him. He wanted to be alone with her at any price.

Her face tilted up as he approached. Beams from the nearest streetlight embraced it in a swathe of highlights and shadows. Her tresses billowed in the night breeze like undulating flames.

Contradictory compulsions wrenched at each other inside him. The need to capture, conquer, and the urge to savor, slow down.

The second impulse won out, forced his feet to stop before they took him all the way pressing her against her car.

He was close enough to reach out and run his fingers through that blazing cascade of hair. He didn't. Somehow. He drew deep of her scent instead, let it permeate him, before he let it escape on a grudging exhalation. "So…you bid one million dollars for an hour with me."

Her shoulders jerked on a dejected shrug. "Yeah. And for the record, I would have doubled the winning bid if I could have."

He inhaled sharply. "You think I'm worth that much?"

"I think you're worth every dollar of your billions."

He bit into his lip. It was either that or drag her to him and bite into hers. As he would. Just not yet. What flowed between them deserved the reward of leisure and thoroughness. But holding back was a punishment, too. One her every word made harder to take. He was used to flattery, could sense falseness and self-interest even in trace quantities. He detected only sincerity from her. Alien urges swamped him, to punch the air, to thump his chest.

He shoved his hands into his pockets so they wouldn't find their way around her. "I do have more hours available apart from the one that other bidder won, you know?"

"Oh. *Oh.* You mean…?"

The surge of hope on her face made him fist his hands in his pockets, emphasizing his—problem. It was either that or snatch them out and pounce on her. "I mean, if you're still interested, I'll take that million-dollar check."

"If?" She coughed. Her eyes tore from his, slammed around, the dazed excitement in them tingling through him on a path that connected his fingertips to his scalp, his loins to his toes. Her gaze settled at her feet. "*There* it is." She dropped down in a crouch, pooling her flowing taffeta skirt on the ground, making her look like a gigantic flower as she retrieved the matching evening bag. She jerked back up, not lingering to look up at him from that position, to milk it for all the sensual promise it could yield.

She didn't need any of that. She needed only to breathe—to be—to exercise maximum effect on him. But it pleased him beyond measure that she didn't operate that way.

She fumbled with her bag, produced her checkbook. He watched as she scribbled furiously with even, beautiful print. Then she tore out the check, extended it to him. "Fill in the beneficiary."

He took it, folded and placed it in his outer pocket before he reached into his inner one, produced his own checkbook and pen.

In a minute he tore a check out, handed it to her. "*I'm* bidding *two* million. Add to that whatever amount you see fit, fill in the total and make it out to whomever you like."

Her movement to take the check felt like a reflex. She didn't look at it, remained gaping at him. "What's this for?"

"The two million is my bid for the time we've had together so far. The amount you'll specify is for the rest of the evening."

"The *whole* evening?"

"And the night."

"The *night?*"

Durante's lips twitched. Her squeaks would have amused him if they weren't pouring fuel on his inflamed senses. She really hadn't thought it a possibility he'd offer this. "If you wish it."

Her blush intensified until she seemed to smolder in the night. And he saw it in his mind's eye in high-definition clarity, himself carrying her to the nearest flat surface to ravish her for that hour she'd bid on, before sweeping her away from the world to do so again for several nights on end.

It was all so surreal he felt he was dreaming it. Yet it was so real it abraded him with its intensity and immediacy. He'd never experienced such a state of distressed arousal. And for him to be in this condition just by looking, imagining… Unbelievable.

At last she spluttered, "Uh…isn't this a bit…you know…?"

He inclined his head. "Too fast? Too soon? You think so?"

A moan-giggle escaped her, another blow to his restraint. "If you think I can think right now, think again."

"Exactly. This isn't about thinking. This is about feeling. About knowing. I know what you make me feel. You made me feel it from the first moment. I wanted more than an hour with you. I want this night, *bellissima,* and as many more as you'll give me."

"That's assuming you'll want more nights after the first…" Her face scrunched into a wince. "Okay, excuse me as I give swallowing my tongue a serious shot."

"With me around to do it? What a waste that would be. And why would you even want to try?"

"Because it sounded as if I was agreeing to share this night with you and was trying to make sure it wouldn't be the one and only."

Every word out of her mouth… He pressed the heel of his palm to his breastbone, as if that would quell the itching behind it. "And you didn't mean that?"

"God, no, I-I…" She threw both hands over her face, before looking up at him, helplessness and accusation filling her expression. "It's your fault. Exposure to you is turning my gray matter into day-old milkshake."

A laugh tore out of him, drove his head back with the force of its unexpectedness and power. "Turnabout is fair play. Although you turn mine into the boiling version." He reduced the distance between them another step, testing his stamina, thrilling to the torture of balancing on the edge of loss of control. "And I will want more nights. As many as I can have. I hope you won't hold back to observe an 'appropriate' period before indulging in intimacy. I want nothing more than to end this night with you in my arms, in my bed."

She melted back against her car. "And I want nothing more than to end this night in both."

Gabrielle watched Durante's eyes flare at her admission, knew he'd reach for her. She had to say the rest now. *Now.*

"But I can't."

The flare subsided, ice putting out the blue-hot flames.

Something twisted beneath her ribs. She couldn't bear to see disappointment replacing exhilaration in his eyes.

She hurtled on. "Believe it or not, I did approach you with business and only business in mind."

Relief swamped her when his eyes simmered again. "I believe you. But it ceased to be business the moment you laid eyes on me."

She didn't even think of denying the fact. "Yes." She still had to qualify it. "But I can't afford to let it be that way—"

He cut across her unsteady words. "You can't afford to let it be any other way. Business will be taken care of in due time. But I'm not postponing this for anything else's sake."

"But what *is* this?"

"Something unknown to either of us, something unprecedented. And you know it as well as I do."

Gabrielle stared at him. He kept stunning her. But what most amazed her was that she picked up no malice from him, that malignant triumph most men transmitted when women made the mistake of not only falling for them, but admitting it, too.

Not him. She felt he was above pettiness and double standards. This was also no line that he gave every desirable woman he met. In fact, his ruthlessness likely originated from his never instigating the pursuit. He was renowned for his detachment.

There was nothing detached about him now. She just knew he was being swept along the same unstoppable current as she was.

That didn't mean she could let herself be swept. There was far more at stake than the elapsing of "an appropriate you're the woman to whom only carte-blanche concessions will do justice."

"God, stop with the impossible-to-live-up-to stuff."

"You've already lived up to all of it by making me feel this way, think this way. So, what's your condition?"

"That you give me back my check."

He didn't hesitate, not in expression, not in action. He produced her check as the words left her lips. Delight fizzed in her blood. He hadn't paused to ponder her intention, trusted that whatever it was, there was nothing underhanded about it.

Her hand trembled as she extended his back to him. "Here's yours. Now I don't owe you untold millions."

He didn't reach for it. "Keep it, *bellissima*. You wouldn't owe me a cent. That's for the causes of your choice."

"Oh, I would owe you. I wanted to make a donation through you, while gaining something for myself. But if I take your check, I would be 'donating' *your* money. So, you donate what you wish and I'll do the same and let's take money out of the equation, start this on a real equal footing."

He took the check. "I'll just keep it until you wish to donate something you can't afford. Now, shall we?"

Her heart began to race her. "Shall we…what exactly?"

"Spend the rest of the evening together. As for the night…I won't push for anything you can't wait to…donate."

Three

Durante leaned back against the railing of his yacht, almost tasting the beauty of his *bellissima* an arm's reach away.

She stood on the first rung, holding on to the railing, arching into the wind, framed against the lit-up Manhattan skyline they were sailing parallel to.

They'd just left port. There was no moon, but stars hung like tiny beacons above her, and beams of light from the yacht's interior stroked her back in gold, flaring fire through the tresses that billowed behind her as if they were powered by her vitality.

Up until a moment ago, he'd kept catching himself bating his breath. He realized why.

Subconsciously, he'd been waiting for something to kick in, that cynicism that had always been an integral part of him. On some level, he expected to be slammed back to a reality that had nothing to do with this state of affinity. Experience—his and others'—kept trying to intrude with warnings that interaction always doused the testosterone-generated spark.

But then, his pleasure in being near her wasn't just about anticipating the pleasures of bedding her, being inside her. He thrilled to her every gesture and glance. Her every word engaged his demanding sense of the absurd, fueled his eagerness for repartee. He'd wondered if the uncontainable drive to possess her painted his reactions to the rest of her in such intensity, or if it was the other way around.

Now he knew. The amalgam that was her was inextricable to his senses, his mind. Physically and mentally, she was a woman the likes of which he'd never dreamed of encountering.

The thrill of their encounter had been escalating, and he'd gladly succumbed to that unprecedented rapport, reveled in the overpowering attraction. And he hadn't even touched her yet.

"This is magic."

He hardened more at her huskily voiced wonder just as he softened, too, inside. "*Si, ciò è magica, bellissima.* You are."

She swung toward him, a smile frolicking across her lips, her eyes glittering with awareness and delight. There was also a touch of mischief. But the emotion that made him struggle not to crush her in his arms was the hint of hesitation—trepidation, even.

Could it be she was wary of him?

No. He knew she trusted him just as instinctively as he did her. So why was she uneasy? Did she suspect that this couldn't be real? That it would end? He didn't share that worry. Not anymore. He couldn't tell her not to worry, but he would show her she had no need to.

She took one hand off the rail, swept her arm in a graceful arc, eloquently encompassing their surroundings. "I meant this. This perfect night, on this enchanting yacht as it sails through the placid ink of the river."

"But take your magic—ours—out of the equation and it would be just another yacht cruise on another pleasant evening."

She sighed, a sound of contentment. "You must be right.

I've been on night cruises before, in great weather. Felt nothing like this."

Before he could revel in her admission, Giancarlo, his all-around right-hand man, caught his eye in the distance.

Durante inclined his head at her. "Are you ready to eat?"

She jumped down from the railing. "I'm ready to dive into the river and catch fish in my teeth."

"Why didn't you say you were hungry?"

She seemed taken aback. "I didn't realize I was."

"I didn't, either. Other hungers overshadowed it."

Delight swelled in his chest at the guilelessness, the unhesitating consent of her gaze and nod.

He wanted to forget his resolve to delay their gratification, knew she wouldn't stop him if he did. But holding back, while chafing, was more gratifying than anything he'd ever done. He gestured for her to precede him, exhilaration shooting through him. She gave a choked laugh and almost skipped ahead.

As they traversed the massive deck to the dining hall, she exclaimed, "Is that *another* swimming pool, under that plexi roof? There was a huge one on the second-level deck."

"Yes, that's the covered one. I'll take you around after I've fed you. You can take a dip in either. I can't offer you something to wear, but you'll be draped in night and wrapped in water, their silk caressing yours unhindered by barriers."

She sped ahead as if to escape his suggestion, muttering, "I'll take a dip-check, thanks."

He chuckled, pointed out another section. "This is where the whirlpools, saunas and Turkish bath are." He pointed to another area. "And *there* are the only modern additions to the yacht's outfitting—a fitness room and comprehensive water sports equipment storage. We can windsurf, water-ski, jet-ski, scuba dive and sail, if you're into any of those."

"I'm into them *all*. I was raised on a Mediterranean island, too, remember? In my opinion, water sports are the ultimate freedom a human being can enjoy. It's been too long since I've had the pleasure."

"You'll never again be deprived of your freedoms and plea-sures, *bellissima*. This yacht and all its facilities are at your disposal to enjoy whenever and however you please."

Her eyes glowed up at him with that light that seemed to shine from inside her. "That's too generous, but I can't—"

"It isn't, and you can and will accept. Say, 'Yes, Durante. I'll do you the honor of considering your yacht my own.'"

Her grimace was at once teasing and moved. "You have the rest of your life to wait? That's how long it will be before I say some-thing like that." He opened his mouth to override her and she rushed to add, "But if your offer stands after tonight, I will take advantage of one or two weekends' windsurfing or jet-skiing."

She still didn't believe this was going to last beyond tonight. He'd have to convince her by action, not words. So he said nothing for now, just smiled down at her.

They were crossing the foyer of the uppermost deck when she turned to him. "When you said 'yacht,' I thought, 'yacht.' Then, when I became certain this floating fortress is where we were headed, I wanted to ask just how you define the word."

His lips twisted. "Yacht-obsessed magazines define this one as the ninth largest private boat in the world. From my specs, it's four hundred feet long with twelve suites of more than six hundred square feet each, not counting the thousand-square-foot master suite. There is also more than eighty thousand square feet of covered and open space."

"Whoa. It's beyond anything I've ever seen and I've been to some exorbitant places. Just this staircase is mind-boggling. I tried to count the steps and got lost."

"Now I feel guilty that I had you climb all one hundred and twenty steps. I should have carried you."

"When I run up to my tenth-floor apartment for exercise? I pick my teeth with a hundred steps." His admiring gaze devoured the results of her hard work. Her constant blush deepened. "This endless balustrade looks like it's made of one piece of solid brass. Which it can't be. Care to explain how it came into being?"

He grinned at her attempt to swerve to safer topics. "It *was* hand-beaten from solid brass by twenty top metal craftsmen who re-created it from remnants of the original balustrade."

She whistled as he seated her at the table that had been set for them. He signaled for Giancarlo to serve dinner right away.

Her eyes panned the huge chamber, lingering on the heavily gilded and embossed wall paneling and the intricately carved and adorned Baroque- and Ottoman-style furniture.

"Everything is so…ornate." She turned to him, her eyes reflecting the flickering candles, that intelligence simmering in her ponderous look. "I somehow didn't think you'd go for something so humongous and elaborate."

"You mean pretentious and gaudy, don't you?"

She didn't seem to give denial a moment's thought. "It is mighty pretentious, though I guess it stops a step shy of gaudy."

He guffawed, loving this. "Everyone I bring on board bursts into raptures extolling my extreme taste. Not you, though."

The look of absolute horror on her face was priceless. "*Maledizione…spiacente…*I'm sorry…" She groaned. "God… I'm so rude."

"You're *candid.* And it goes straight to my head. You're also right. There's nothing here that appeals to me, either. But this yacht was my mother's. It was her father's gift to her on her marriage. He was flaunting his wealth, wanting to prove he was on par with the king his daughter married. He named the boat *La Regina del Mare,* to underline my mother's new royal status. He also wished her to keep the Boccanegra family name and old-world nobility in the minds and envies of the jet-set, the new world's aristocracy. But she had no interest in that and sent the boat to languish at the docks of Napoli, where it fell into disrepair.

"After her death I renamed it *Angelica* for her, commissioned its restoration to its exact former glory, which I didn't have the vaguest recollection of. I regretted my act the moment I stepped on board the finished product. But even with its...excessive size and interiors, I discovered I loved living on board and roving the seas. I thought to re-outfit it to my needs and tastes, but I decided to leave it as is. Eventually I will donate it as a museum in my mother's memory, one that can be rented for huge sums that will go to the charities I founded in her name. I'm in the process of buying another yacht that doesn't scream 'party animal.'"

She sighed with the satisfaction of someone who'd been listening to a poignant tale. "Which is just about the last thing you are."

"*Sì*. The sporadic sponsored charity event is the limit of my social mingling." He only then noticed that Giancarlo must have served their entrées. "Which must be why the etiquette my mother struggled to infuse me with as a small child has rusted from disuse. *Andare avanti*...go ahead, please. I'll talk and you eat."

She immediately pounced on her plate, snatched up one of the golden, crisp lobster puffs. "I thought you'd never ask."

He chuckled, shaking his head at his all-out reaction, started to eat himself. "So tell me...what made you move to Sardinia and/or Italy when you were five?"

She chewed, moaned in enjoyment, beamed at him. "I thought it was you talk and I eat. Lucky for you *my* mother never succeeded in teaching me not to eat and talk at the same time." She reached for a second puff. "About the move—gotta say outside influences helped me make that decision. Like my parents hauling me there."

"*Ragazza difettosa.*" His no-touching-yet rule was growing difficult. His hands ached to smooth those glowing cheeks, cup them and dip his tongue in those tormenting dimples and smile grooves. "You must know where I want to haul you." Her eyes all but groaned *Yes, please.* He inhaled, reminded himself of his resolve. "So why did *they* haul you there?"

She reached for her champagne flute, her eyes losing heat and brightness. "It's a convoluted story. I think it started with my father's business in the States having many outlets in Italy and the surrounding Mediterranean islands. He went bankrupt around the time I was five. He also suffered from depression. In the years following his death, I've often asked my mother if she thought that influenced the decisions that led to his bankruptcy, or if it was the other way around. Not that I expected an answer, or thought it would make a difference."

"When did he die?" He watched her put down the puff. It was clear her appetite was gone. He groaned. "Don't answer that."

The surprise in her eyes seemed directed at her own reaction, not his words. "No, I-I want to tell you. He died when I was eleven."

He gritted his teeth, hating to see her suffer echoes of the anguish the child she'd been must have felt. "You were old enough to be aware of all the problems going on around you then."

She nodded. "I was."

"It still haunts you."

She put down her glass unsteadily. "It's not fun remembering nothing of my father but a man buried under so much gloom and despair. I try to cling to memories of the man he was beneath all that, but they're rare. During those times he was wonderful, which makes it all more painful, knowing how much of him was wasted. Remembering how angry I was at him doesn't help, either. I've since realized that he couldn't help his condition, but try to convince a kid of that. I blamed him for his moods, his inaccessibility. And later on, I blamed myself for that blame."

Everything she said struck chords inside him. He'd suffered something very similar. "Where was your mother during all that?"

She started to eat again, an adorably determined look on her face. "Struggling to protect me from the torment festering within Dad as it spread out to engulf us, and to keep him from disintegrating while not succumbing herself under the burdens thrown on the so-called 'healthy adult' in this setup."

"You have a good relationship with her."

She swallowed her mouthful convulsively, her eyes tearing up. "I had the best relationship a girl could hope for with her mother. She died seven months ago."

He ached to stop this, to spare her reliving her anguish. But he felt she'd refuse to abandon the subject. She more than wanted to tell him. It felt as if she needed to. He wanted to give her anything she needed. He asked quietly, "How?"

"Sh-she had rheumatoid arthritis. A severe condition. Then, during a regular checkup, she was diagnosed with stage-four pancreatic cancer. She was dead within two months."

"You were with her when she passed away?"

She nodded. "She didn't live here with me, because her condition deteriorated whenever she left the Mediterranean climate. I went to her every minute I could. When we knew there was no hope of remission, she wanted to live at home. I wanted to be the one to take care of her, so I moved into her villa. I'd taken paramedic courses and administered the palliative measures that were all that could be done until…until the end."

"You had medical supervision during that time?"

She bit her lip, hard. "Her doctor was on call and two nurses came twice a day to check on my measures."

"And they found everything to their satisfaction."

"It was easy to get it right. There wasn't much to be done."

"Yet you're still afraid you messed up those simple measures, didn't give the mother you loved—who trusted you to take care of her during her last days—the best care."

He saw shock rip through her, as if he'd reached inside and yanked out her heart. Then, to his horror, her face crumpled, her teary eyes spilling over. "Sometimes I wake at night crying, terrified I gave her a wrong painkiller dose, that she was in agony and bearing it as usual, that I made her make the wrong decision in going home. That she died suffering because of me."

Battling their physical need was one thing. But *this* need, for solace, he was powerless against. He hadn't offered or sought comfort since childhood. He had to offer it now, seek it. To and from her.

He exploded to his feet, came around to her, pulled her up.

The moment she filled his arms, it was as if things were uprooted inside him. Separateness. Seclusion.

This. He'd been waiting for this. This woman. This connection. And he'd never known he'd been waiting.

She lay her head against his heart and trembled. He stroked her hair as he'd longed to from the first moment. It was beyond anything his imagination had spun. And so was what he felt for her. He wanted her to let go, give him all her resurrected misery to bear. He wanted her to pour out the rest. He was certain she'd never unburdened herself.

He prodded her to give him all. "Why did your father take you to Sardinia when his business collapsed? Was he going home?"

"No." She sniffed, stirred, her eyes beseeching him to resume normalcy. He complied, let her go, somehow, seated her, went back to his chair, signaled for Giancarlo to serve the main course.

She stalled, tasting her lobster in lime butter sauce, asking Giancarlo about the recipe. When she ran out of delaying tactics, was in control again, she began talking. "Dad had a friend who asked him to relocate us there so he could help, which he couldn't do effectively if we lived thousands of miles away."

"And did he? Help?"

"Above and beyond. He paid off Dad's debts, tried endlessly to put him back on his feet. But no matter what he did, Dad kept spiraling downward. This friend even took care of us after he died, financed my education until I graduated."

"And you didn't like that. Even though you liked the man."

"God, how do you keep working out how I feel? Do you read minds?" She groaned. "But of *course* you do. You wouldn't be you if you didn't." Before he could tell her it was only her he was so attuned to, she went on. "Yeah, I love him. But I hated feeling so helpless, so indebted. I worked, paid my rent and expenses, but he was adamant about not letting me get a tuition loan. I only accepted when he promised he'd let me pay him back."

"But he was only humoring you so you'd accept."

"Your insight is uncanny, isn't it? You realized at once what I only realized when I got a great paying job and demanded to repay him only for him to—surprise—refuse to take a cent."

"But you drilled your way into making him take it, *giusto?*"

"*Assolutamente giusto*…dead right. I bet he finally took the money so he'd hear the end of it. Not that that was the end of it. When my mom finally gave me a real idea of the magnitude of our family's debt to him, I became consumed with the need to repay it all, so I'd feel free, and she would, too."

"And I bet you managed to pay it all back."

Her lashes fluttered down again. "Eventually, yes."

"And that cost you. What did it cost you, *bellissima?*"

Her lips twisted in something too much like self-loathing. "Marrying the worst possible man."

The world stopped. His heart followed. "You're *married?*"

Her eyes slammed back to his, enormous with alarm and agitation. "*No.* I'm divorced. Six years ago now. *Grazie a Dio.*"

His heart attempted to restart, lurched and clanged against the insides of a chest that felt lined with thorns. "Was he rich?"

She winced. "Filthy."

"Like me?"

"Uh, no. Your wealth transcends filthiness into obscenity."

He couldn't reciprocate her tremulous attempt to lighten things up. "You married him so he'd repay your family's debts?"

"Actually, it was his idea. I was his PA and he heard me on the phone with my mom and used it as another pressure tactic."

"He needed to? You weren't attracted to him?"

"I felt nothing beyond unease that I couldn't reciprocate his interest. But the job was great, so I kept hoping he'd find someone else. He didn't, kept pointing out that I didn't, either, that maybe I can't feel…passion, which was okay because love stories never end well, anyway. I began to think he was right, as I knew nothing of what makes a relationship work or what a man who'd make a good husband was like. Compared to my father, he seemed like the essence of stability. And he made a solid case for a marriage between us built on mutual respect and realistic expectations."

He barely stopped himself from snarling. "He conned you."

"Oh, no. I decided to disregard my reservations, my lack of feelings for him, followed the lure of paying off my family's debts in one chunk. I dug my own grave by being so mercenary."

He snarled now. "You were nothing of the sort. *He* was the conniving bastard. If he felt *anything* for you, he would have freed you from debt and left it up to you to take him or not."

"That would have only transferred my debt to him, and I would have felt honor-bound to marry him anyway."

"He could have made it clear that there would have been no debt, or offered that you repay it in installments."

"I did insist on including the condition in the prenups that our funds be separate and whatever he loaned me I'd return."

"And he pounced on those terms," he bit off. "You were what? Twenty? Twenty-one? And how old was he?"

"I was twenty-three. He was thirty-nine. And a widower."

"He *did* con you. He convinced you to consider it a business deal in which pros outweigh cons, pretended he was satisfied with that. Until he got his hands on you." Her shrug was loud with concession. He wanted to slam his fists down on the table. "And he didn't pay off your debts."

"How did you…? Oh, OK. I did say I married the worst man."

"Actually, you said paying your debt cost you marrying said man. Most would assume that he did pay it. But I'd bet my fortune he didn't. I know that because I know users, and that man was beyond that. He kept after you to break your resistance, but instead of building anticipation as he pursued you, he built up antipathy, planned to wreak vengeance on you as soon as he had you in his power." He caught her hand, pressed it. "I only wish to God the extent of his aggression was the passive breaking of the pact he never meant to keep. But he didn't stop there, did he?" She shook her head. "He abused you. Verbally, mentally." The last word seemed to cut him as it came out. "Sexually."

She stared at him again as if he'd torn her open and looked inside, distress brimming with the shock of exposure, with the misplaced shame of the victim.

At last she gave a choking gulp. A mortified nod admitted his insight. "I bought his excuses, his blame, for four months. I didn't love him, he was frustrated, yadda yadda. Then he…he…"

"He hit you."

She lurched. Her chest heaved. With a sharp inhalation, she muttered, "He put me in the hospital."

Four

Durante had never considered himself a violent man.

Now, as he stared down at her bent head, murderous aggression took hold of his every nervous transmission. Need boiled his blood—to defend her in retrospect, to avenge her, to torture and cripple that vermin who'd hurt her.

Words left his lips in a vicious staccato. "Tell me you reported him and he's now serving time."

"Uh, no…actually, I didn't." He heard something rumbling, vaguely realized the sound was issuing from him. She rushed in to add, "But he didn't get the chance to come near me again. I started divorce proceedings before I even reached the hospital."

He glared at her, his brain seeming to expand in the confines of his skull with the brutal buildup of anger, the inability to vent it. At least not yet. He *would* pay that man back.

She suddenly shut her eyes. "Okay, let's rewind and replay before I dig a hole to Malaysia. I made it all sound so pathetic and self-pitying, and that isn't how I see my life. I've had it way better than most people. Despite my father's problems, so many things, starting with my mother and our benefactor, provided me with a secure and reasonably happy childhood. I had a great time at boarding school and college, and my marriage, ugliness and all, lasted only four months and I own up to my role in it. I've established my own company and I loved every second of exploring and achieving so much on the way. My mother died, but I'm thankful she didn't suffer long and that I had such an incredible friend and parent for so long. So...I hope I haven't caused you to reach your whining tolerance level."

She was making light of her ordeals, and, *maledizione,* meaning it. The expectedness of her last words awoke his humor, which he thought an insult to the suffering she'd related. But her come-on, laugh-with-me expression forced him to submit.

He coughed a distressed laugh. "You sent my sense of perspective levels through the roof, after they'd dwindled to trace elements. You forced me to revise how I perceive my own life. Seems I've been guilty of letting my...issues rule my mind-set."

She shook her head, teasing radiating from her heavenly eyes. "I thought higher beings like you had global obstacles and dilemmas and crises, but nothing so petty as 'issues.'"

He gave a grunt laden with self-disgust. "Leave it to you to underline how oblivious and tiny and self-indulgent it all is."

She chuckled. "Anytime."

He reached out across the table, took her hand. He needed to be connected to her as he made his own confessions. "My experience with my mother reflects yours with your father. She died five years ago, but I too was eleven when I started to realize I was losing her. It was then that I set out to detach myself, that I learned that no one is guaranteed to be there for me. I've become so comfortable being disconnected, so driven and distracted, that I no longer notice all the good that fills my life."

Her other hand descended to his, imbuing him with a calm

that was previously unknown to him, a restfulness to mirror the compassion that filled her eyes. "She suffered depression, too?"

He'd never discussed this, never given what his mother had suffered a name, not even with his siblings. He needed to talk about it now, with her, needed to name what had taken his mother away a piece every day, look it full in the face instead of evading it and having it invade far more of him instead.

"I think she was bipolar. Severely so."

"So it's true. No one is exempt. My father, a man who had everything, your mother, a queen with the world at her feet, both prisoners to something so dark and inescapable inside them."

Pressure built behind his eyes as cold outrage at the injustice of it all gave way to the empathy flowing between them in sweeping currents. He surrendered to the release of sharing, of having another fully appreciate and understand.

Suddenly, urgency stained her gaze. Everything inside him became primed to defend, to contain. He had no tolerance for her distress, he was discovering. "What is it, *bellissima?* Tell me."

She grimaced. "It's nothing. It's…" She stopped, closed her eyes, exhaled. "What the hell. I've put my foot in it too much already to get delicate at this late stage. I was just wondering if… if you've ever wondered if you have that seed of sourceless desperation and instability inside you?"

He stiffened with yet another jolt at how in tune she was with him, sensing fears that never came into focus, but cast their darkness over his existence nevertheless.

He let his counter-question acknowledge her insight just as it expressed his concern for her. "Do you?"

"Only since my mother died. I finally wondered if I've never been able to be close to others because I had something lurking inside me, because I subconsciously felt that emotional involvement would raise the chances that it would manifest."

"And what's your verdict?"

"I don't know. What complicates matters and stops me from

coming up with anything conclusive is the fact that it wasn't a struggle not to be close. I wasn't even tempted until…"

She stopped. He couldn't anymore. He cupped her cheek as he'd been aching to. "Until tonight."

Warmth surged from his gut when she acquiesced, to the truth of his statement, to his hold, letting her flesh mold to his palm.

And he had to ask. "Did you ever wonder if whatever consumed your father wasn't sourceless, after all?"

She nuzzled into his caress. "I guess *sourceless* is the wrong word to use, what with all the physiological and social factors involved in the development of such a major disorder. I guess it's the out-of-proportion, ever-compounding emotional response that becomes so far removed from whatever triggered it, making it seem as if there were no origin." She sighed, singeing his flesh with the heat of her breath. "As I said, I'll never know what started my father down that spiral."

"I know what started my mother down hers. It was my father."

Such shock, such pain flooded her eyes at his muttered bitterness that he groaned, cupped her head, needing to alleviate her distress.

She reached out to his face, her hand trembling in a caress that assuaged some of the darkness festering inside him.

She finally said, "I'm so sorry you believe that. I can't imagine how painful it is to think one of your parents was responsible for the other's deterioration. It's the only thing that holds me together, that I believe that there was no one to blame."

He rose, bent across the table. He gazed into her misty eyes for a heart-thudding moment, then descended, pressed his lips to hers in a brief, barely leashed kiss. *"Grazie, bellissima."*

Her moan reverberated inside him. His fingers fisted in her tresses, spilling another moan from her lips, detonating charges of sensation across his skin. He withdrew before temptation overwhelmed him, sat down. His gaze pored over her, the image of her beauty burned onto his retinas.

Such beauty. Totally her own, following no one else's ideas or rules, including his own before he'd set eyes on her. Beyond physical, with so many levels to it—levels he kept discovering with no end in sight. She was short-circuiting the civilized man he'd been certain he was, unleashing a primal male who wanted to possess, plunder. But it also made that same male want to protect, to pamper.

She inclined her head at him. "You can sing, can't you?"

He blinked at the question—the statement, really. He didn't even think to inquire about such a detour's origin and intent. He just flowed with her along the wave of unpredictability, of freedom from rules and expectations.

"Can't everyone," he said. "to some degree or another?"

"Uh, no. Not according to my singing teacher, another suffering soul who told me she had nightmares of waking up in a world where everyone had my same singing ability, making her profession obsolete and putting her permanently out of a job."

He frowned. "*My* teacher criticized my intentional truancy. He wouldn't have disparaged my performance or made me feel responsible for it had it been a limitation on my part. That inconsiderate wretch who taught you had no business telling a child something like that, just because your talents didn't meet her standards and your progress didn't conform to her timetable."

She beamed him such a look, full of mischief and embarrassment, that he wondered where he found the will to remain where he was. "Uh, I wasn't exactly a child when the brilliant idea of taking singing lessons sprouted in my mind three years ago. And I did test her last tune-sensitive nerve by insisting on singing along with Whitney Houston and Maria Callas. The comparison was agonizing even to my own self-forgiving ears. But I have a feeling you can hold your own with the Elvises and Pavarottis of the world."

He raised one eyebrow, goading her into telling him more. "Hmm, I wonder how you came by that conviction."

Her grin grew impish and indulgent at once. "In your case, fishing will get you whales. You reaffirm that conviction every time you open your mouth and unleash that honed weapon you have for a voice. *Uomo cattivo* that you are, you unrepentantly use it to its full destructive effect. It's very easy for me to imagine you taking your mastery over it to its highest conclusion."

Stimulation revved higher. He let himself revel in the gratification of their repartee, challenged, fishing for even bigger whales. "I've heard many superlative singers who don't sound special when they talk."

"Sure, but I bet that's not the case with you."

"So what are you after? An admission? An audition?"

Her dimples flashed at him. "The first would be great, so I can gloat over my uncanny acumen. The second, alas, would be so much better even than having your ear for an hour—or a week—that I think it would warrant something larger than a ten-million-dollar bid."

He reached for her hand and placed it on her fork. "I have a third option. Let's finish this meal, and I'll offer you something better than either at no cost but your willingness to accept it." She sat forward, anticipation ablaze on her face. And he offered something he'd never imagined offering to anyone, ever. "A serenade."

Darkness was melting under dawn's advance, the horizon starting to simmer with colors, the rest of the sky's blackness bleaching to indigo, the stars blinking out one by one.

Durante had taken his *bellissima* to the bow, initiating a match of quips around the *Titanic* movie parallel. Merriment had dissolved with the night into a silence filled with serenity and companionship. Soon it seemed as natural and needed as breathing for her to fill his embrace, just as she seemed to need to be contained there.

For the next hour, as the magic of the night segued into the new spell of dawn, he encompassed her, her back to his front, his arms crisscrossed around her midriff, his legs parted to accommodate her, imbuing her with his heat, protecting her from the chill of the breeze. She accepted him as her shield, surrendered to his cosseting and to that of the wind on her face as the yacht sailed toward the sun.

In this proximity, there was no disguising the extent of his arousal. Not that he tried to. He'd admitted his reaction to her minutes into their first conversation. His body had made its own admissions to her the moment he gathered her to him, his erection obvious through the confines of clothes and control.

Her own state must be as acute. The only movements she seemed capable of were the spasmodic pressing of her hands on the railing, and trembling. Was she trying not to press back into him as hard as he wanted to grind into her?

But he wouldn't fracture this intensity, this purity of feeling for anything. This was too rare to rush, too precious to squander even for the ecstasy they were certain to find in each other. Not yet. They had to have this first.

It was magnificent, sharing this with her, experiencing each other without words after the liveliness of their verbal communication. Now the only sounds that permeated the whispers and whistles of the wind and the splash of the water were his groans as he pressed his lips into her neck, against her cheeks, the corner of her mouth, her moans as her tremors spiked with every press and glide. He felt as if every inch of her was made to click into every inch of him, that the eight or nine inches he had on her five foot six or seven had been bestowed on him so he'd envelop her like this.

Then she turned her head, turned up eyes glittering with the wonder of what they'd shared since they'd met twelve hours or a forever ago, whispered, *"Ora, per favore."*

Now, please. Indeed. So this was it. The moment of truth.

He'd never sung in another's presence. Not since primary

school, anyway. And he was about to sing to this enchanted creature who'd appeared out of nowhere and made him forget everything, his exhaustion, his wariness. The world.

He let his arms tighten around her for a moment before he stepped away. Then he went down on one knee.

A sharp gasp tore from her. Then, with another distressed sound, she swooped down, tried to pull him up.

He tangled his hands into her hair, tugged gently, brought her down for another of those fleeting, tormenting kisses.

Then, as his lips clung to hers, he breathed the first line of Caruso. *"Qui dove il mare luccica, e tira forte il vento…"*
Here where the sea sparkles and the wind is blowing…

She bolted up, severing the last clinging touch between their lips, and staggered back to lean limply against the railing, her eyes stricken, her lips parting on choppy puffs.

He remained kneeling at her feet, giving his voice full rein as he continued to sing the song he'd only ever memorized because he felt like he was soaring when he let his voice ride the beauty and power of the melody, never giving a moment's thought to the lyrics. Now the lyrics seemed to have been written so that he could describe these moments with her. They took on meanings their writer hadn't intended, poured into the mold of the moment.

Then he came to the refrain, and that, most of all, resonated with the exact expressions that crowded inside him, let the passion she'd aroused in him take shape and sound and flow with the fervor of the timeless words.

"Te voglio bene assai, ma tanto tanto bene sai. È una catena ormai, che scioglie il sangue dint'e vene sai…"
I want you so much, I truly want you so much it's now like a shackle that melts the blood inside the veins, you know…

Tears gushed from her eyes, and her face shuddered with too many emotions to follow, let alone fathom. She seemed in pain.

Alarm and suspicion crashed inside his head. What if this

song provoked raw memories, if he'd managed, not to please her, woo her, but to upset her? He surged to his feet. He couldn't stop his arms from gathering her to him until he had her off the ground and in his safekeeping.

"Durante…please…" The quivering of her voice augmented his alarm, made him hold her away so he could ascertain her state, apologize, divert her agitation. His gut clenched, now he grimaced as he saw her lips working before he realized they were forming a tremulous smile. "Please…don't stop."

His whole body slackened with relief.

She swayed when he set her back on her feet, gripped his arms, eagerness blazing on her face. "Please, please keep singing. I thought I could imagine how incredible you'd sound, but it seems even my imagination is tone-deaf."

He guffawed. There was no way he could ever predict what she'd say next. "If so, how do you know if I sound incredible or not?"

"Oh, my 'difficulties' lie in tone reproduction, not recognition. And then this…" She waved both hands at him, before taking them both to her chest to press her heart in a gesture so moved and moving he groaned. "…transcends hearing. Please—sing."

He plastered her against him, no longer restraining his urgency, one hand dipping below her corset-like top to bask in her firm softness and heat, the other digging into her mane, turning her face up for his worshipping. And he sang.

The liberation, the exhilaration was indescribable. To cut the tethers of separateness and wariness and propriety, to let himself go, let his voice boom with passion, break with poignancy. The storm of emotions and expressions that raged on her face with every note, the tears of acute enjoyment that streamed, were the purest form of adulation he'd ever had, the only he craved having.

When the last vibrato died away, she was panting, then she

flung herself at him, pressed her wet face into his chest, until he felt her fervor practically eating through it, her essence permeating it. "*Grazie,* Durante. *Molto, molto grazie.*"

It was a long time before either of them stirred. It was she who moved, casting stunned looks around, before looking up at him sheepishly. "It's morning."

"*Sì,* that's what usually follows dawn, I hear," he teased.

Something warm danced in her eyes. "I wouldn't know. I'm no expert on dawn or how long it takes to break. I'm always in a coma from one until seven a.m."

"So this is your first time staying up all night?"

"It's my first time…for just about everything."

There was no doubt in his mind that was the truth. There was no thought of hiding how he felt in return. "*Sì.* For me, too."

The blast of delight in her clear-again eyes made him feel limitless, swathed everything in new meanings and depths. He basked in it all until contrition entered her expression. "I kept you up all night on a work day."

He waved it off. "Why did I strive so hard to be where I am if not for the flexibility of forging my own timetable?"

"Who're you kidding? You crack the whip over your own head harder than you do over anybody else's."

He guffawed again, loving this. "Very subtle way of saying I'm a slave driver. One with a fetish for self-flagellation."

"I bet you didn't become who you are by being flexible with your time and taking days off."

"To put your mind to rest on the sacrifice of my taking a day off, I can afford to in this instance, because before we met I put in thirty-six hours of work, more than covering for it in advance."

"Oh, God…that means you've been awake for forty-eight hours now. And I kept you up all night yakking and singing and…and…"

"And being tormented within an inch of my sanity? Laughing my head off? Confessing my darkest secrets? Being fully alive?"

"Yeah…uh…all that," she croaked. "But I bet you were longing to hit the sheets."

"The only sheets I want to hit are those with you spread out on them. Being with you has been the most worthwhile reason to forgo sleep that I've ever had. I never realized there was anything to want as fiercely as I want a steady supply of sleepless nights with you."

She stared up at him, motionless, breathless. Then the first tremor broke through the stillness. The second merged into a stream that shook her. Gratification swelled, that he affected her to that extent. He might not be exhibiting the same outward manifestation, but she shook him, too, to the core.

He embraced her again, absorbed her tremors. They were her response to him made tangible. They belonged to him. He wanted them, along with everything that made her herself.

He'd given Giancarlo orders to keep sailing until he told him otherwise. He wanted to keep on sailing, never to return her to her life, never to return to his.

He was thinking she'd say yes if he proposed that radical plan when she raised an agitated face, whispered, "Take me home, please, Durante."

Five

Durante raised an eyebrow at Gabrielle's TriBeCa apartment building's concierge in response to his open surprise and curiosity. Very strange reaction coming from someone whose job description was headed by discretion and diplomacy.

Did the man recognize him? Or was it his tenant's return dressed in an evening gown in broad daylight, escorted by a strange man?

He did see recognition in the man's eyes. Which *wasn't* strange. Royalty was an endless source of public fascination and romanticizing anywhere in the world. But it was far more so in the States, especially in New York, his adopted home for the last five years. It seemed New Yorkers clamored for anything that would transport them from their hectic lives. Being a prince of an exotic kingdom, combined with his vast wealth, was the stuff of fairy tales to them. That this view did not match the reality of his life had nothing to do with their perception of it. The perception was there to stay.

So the man recognized him. But Durante was still convinced his second interpretation of his reaction was the correct one. Which led to another conviction. The incident had so surprised the man because he hadn't seen her coming home with a man before. She'd told the truth about first times. As he knew she had.

Not that he was "coming home" with her. He was taking her to her door, had no idea if she'd invite him in.

She'd asked him to take her home after he'd again stressed his open-ended desire, had barely spoken during the ride there. Considering how fluent she'd been up until then, her fraught silence had disturbed him more by the minute. He'd tried to tell himself she was exhausted, that not everyone was an insomniac able to function on sporadic half hours of sleep. But what if this night hadn't meant as much to her as it had to him? What if she'd decided that it wasn't prudent to let things develop further?

The sharp *ping* of the elevator as they reached her tenth-floor apartment cut through his oppressive thoughts. He let her precede him, fell into step with her through the dimly lit corridor leading to her corner apartment, his hand gripping hers as if he were afraid she'd dematerialize. Then they reached her door.

It was the same as all the others. It was also the gateway to the one place on earth he wanted to be.

Behind this door lay the stage of her unseen existence. Where she walked barefoot, dressed and undressed, reflected, shed tears. Where she sang in out-of-tune abandon as she cooked her meals, danced in front of mirrors to snippets of music that blipped inside her head, washed away exhausting days under the spray of hot water, drowned her angers and anxieties in steaming baths and surrendered to oblivion after a book dropped from her hand at the strike of 1 a.m.... or after she'd pleasured herself.

Crossing this door into that microcosm became his highest goal. To be allowed into her sanctuary, to be given the privilege to witness her secrets, see to her safety, cater to her needs.

She turned, her eyes overflowing with so much emotion that his mind seized. Then her whisper floated in the silence, impeded, unsteady.

"I wanted to be on my turf when I said this. I-I…"

She was going to say goodbye. *No.* He couldn't let her. "Don't say anything now, *bellissima.* Just get some sleep. When you've taken it all in, let me see you again. We'll take it from there."

Her gaze wavered, then she groaned. "God, I'm so stupid. You must be exhausted. Oh, just go please…"

He caught her arm, stopped her babbling. "The last thing I need now is sleep. What did you want to say? If it's anything other than 'I don't think this should go any farther,' please say it."

Her flush rose. His whole body bunched as her lips parted on a hectic inhalation and she burst out, "I want this night, Durante. Or this day. Or whenever we are. And I want as many nights and days as I can ha—"

Durante couldn't wait for her confession to finish exiting her lips before he devoured it along with them. The way she met his ardor halfway with as much ferocity told him everything he needed to know. This time there was no hesitation on her part, as there was no intention of holding back on his.

He stilled the tremors invading the fullness of her lower lip in a bite that made her cry out, arch into him, all lushness and surrender. The taste and feel and scent of her eddied in his arteries, pounded through his system. Her urgency spilled into his mouth in moans and gasps that blanked his mind. He gathered her thighs through the layers of cloth, raised her, opened her for his bulk, pinned her to her door with the force of his hunger. His tongue drove inside her as his erection thrust against her heat through layers of barriers, losing rhythm in the wildness.

Her tongue slid against his, rubbed, tangled, her lips suckled at his, her teeth matching him nip for nip until he slammed against her, rattling the door, the wall that housed it.

This—as she called it—was everything. It couldn't be

spoiled, could only deepen and widen and intensify. This wasn't rushing things, wasn't too soon. This was how it should be. They didn't need time to know this was right. It was. Time would only provide the leisure to explore and savor all the ways of how right it was.

But this totality of response was also frightening. His grip on control was softening, the need to ram inside her, here, now, ride her until she convulsed around him, drenched his flesh with her pleasure and he pumped her full of his, was replacing his mental faculties. And that was after just a kiss.

But it wasn't a kiss. It was a rehearsal for their mating, enough to portray what that would be like. Something so outside the realm of his experience he couldn't even begin to imagine it.

He knew that on a fundamental level. He had to know the rest.

He tore his lips from the lock of her passion, shuddered with her cry, her lurch, her demand that he resume their fusion.

He molded her features with his mouth as if mapping them into tactile memory. "Tell me your name, *bellissima*. I need to know it now, to whisper it into your lips and against your every pleasure point. I need to think it, have it fill my mind as I look on your beauty. I want to roar it as I fill you."

"Gabrielle…" Her moan penetrated his brain, lodged in his erection. Gabrielle. *Yes.* Laced with femininity and strength and complexity. It fit her. But then she'd make any name exceptional, magical. "Gabrielle Williamson."

Everything decelerated as her full name sank into his mind. Then it hit bottom, detonated like a depth mine.

Gabrielle Williamson. The woman who'd recently approached him with an offer he'd refused, as he had dozens of similar ones.

She hadn't accepted "not interested" for an answer, had contacted just about everyone who had an in with him to secure face time with him. He'd heard from many on her behalf, but it was one of his associates who'd finally roused his curiosity. Gerald Whittaker, as shrewd a businessman as they came, had said she was confident her offer was one he couldn't refuse. When he'd said that he'd heard the Don Corleone line too many times for it to work, Gerald had had every confidence himself that she must be on to something Durante would want to know about, that he should at least give her a chance.

Out of respect for Gerald's opinion, he almost had. He'd also wondered what kind of woman had such a rock so taken with her.

But he hadn't agreed to meet her. Because he'd found out exactly what kind of woman she was. The most casual background check had returned a screaming verdict. *Don't let her within a mile of you.*

So he hadn't. Not because he'd believed himself in any danger from the femme fatale whose favorite snack was billionaires. He'd been disgusted by the picture he'd put together. Of her stringing Gerald around, using him to get to an even bigger prey. *Him.* The offer he couldn't refuse would have been the pleasure of having her, no doubt. She'd have been confident that he, like dozens before him, would succumb once she had him in range of her charms. He'd fleetingly entertained agreeing to her panted-after meeting, just to get the message across that *he* could snack on women like her. If he was into junk food.

He shouldn't have been so smug. He should have known that she'd have more cards to play. And she'd played them. Played him. And how. She'd reinvented her approach, hit from another angle. And she'd struck the bull's-eye. He hadn't only proved himself susceptible to her wiles, but he also must have been her easiest quarry ever.

Gabrielle Williamson. *She* was the woman with whom he'd spent the most revitalizing, enthralling time of his life, a time he'd planned never to end. The woman who'd made him forget exhaustion and every preconception about himself and what he could feel. The woman who was wrapped around him, her flesh feeling as if it were as vital to him as his own.

She dragged his face back down to hers, whimpering at his momentary withdrawal. It *had* been only a moment since the lips claiming his had formed the name that had sent reality crashing into him. It had taken only a moment to plunge him from the heights of delight to the depths of disillusion.

His whole being in revolt, he tried to pull back, but she wouldn't let him. She tightened her vise around his body, his will, her ragged whispers of desire impaling his brain, causing another geyser of response to erupt inside him.

So what if she wasn't the unique woman for whom he'd broken all his rules, was instead a siren who came with a warning ignored at the price of defamation and destruction? It should change nothing. His body was reaching critical mass, demanding hers. And she was offering…everything. He should drag her inside, throw her to the ground and take it all. *Then* walk away.

Disillusionment bellowed its bitterness over the flames of desire. It wasn't powerful enough to douse them. Only agony might be.

It tore him apart to think of it all reduced to…this. Rutting. Sexual release. He wanted the unprecedented passion, the sublime emotions along with the all-consuming lust.

But those had all been an illusion. She was everything he abhorred and despised. Nothing like what she'd projected so seamlessly all night. How had she done it? How had she misled his senses to this extent? How had she imbued herself with a vibe that had been so attuned to his? How had she been able to assume a nature so alien to her own? To project characteristics she couldn't begin to understand, let alone have?

The answer to all that was obvious. She was a chameleon. A black widow. A cold-blooded predator.

"Durante, *te voglio bene assai…*"

Her words echoed the ones he'd sung—*sung*—to her. They ripped into him, made him go rigid with the spike of arousal.

For a suspended moment, he let her overwhelm his reason, let himself surrender to the need to forget caution, to deny his realizations. But the very loss of the control finally hurt enough to ignite the deep freeze of rage.

He was just another quarry to her. One she'd gambled she could capture if she got close enough. And he wouldn't let her win. Not even if he was dying to let her. Especially because he was.

He tore her arms off his body, feeling as if they'd taken off strips of his own skin.

Still oblivious to his awakening, she cupped his face, her own etched with her *coup de grâce,* an expression that would have brought him to his knees if he hadn't realized the truth. Total trust, full surrender. Temptation thundered through him.

He staggered away in self-disgust.

This time when he recoiled, he broke free from the prison of her thighs, dropped her back on her own feet. She stumbled, crashed back against the door.

Panic flashed in her eyes. His heart stampeded. Had his involuntary force frightened her, brought back memories of when another man had used his superior strength to hurt her?

Dio, what was he *thinking?* This was an *act.* Her sob story about the husband who'd abused her—the husband she'd used and destroyed instead—had been a string of masterfully composed lies.

Sure enough, the panic was turning to an uncanny emulation of pained confusion, then dread. "Durante…what's wrong?"

Everything, he wanted to roar. *You, the woman, the treasure I thought I found, doesn't exist.*

He glared at her, everything he wanted to yell frothing inside him. His body quaked as if on the verge of explosion.

Then, after a long moment filled with labored-breathing,

without another word or glance, he turned on his heel and walked away.

He wouldn't look back. Ever again. The dream was over.

Gabrielle stood plastered to her door, watching Durante walk away.

She couldn't breathe. Something sharp and burning had lodged in her gut, twisting her to shreds, coagulating into a mass of pain.

A wave of darkness swamped her.

She stumbled around, pressed her clammy face to her door, fumbled inside her purse. Key. Get inside. Damned if she would faint out here. She'd given the tabloids enough fodder for a decade. This would see her to her grave.

Then she was inside. Alone. As she should have remained, as she would from now on. She'd never let anyone close again, never...

All her nerves seemed to snap. She went down in a heap on the ground, her dress swirling around her like a suffocating vortex.

She tore at it. Couldn't bear the oppression. Had to breathe.

It took forever. Then she was in her panties, staggering up and to her bedroom. She fell onto her bed, folded into a ball of anguish. Her body was still throbbing, demanding him... *Stop it.*

Misery engulfed her, wrung her, first with dry heaves, then with tears so violent she thought she might dissolve, dissipate.

She'd thought she'd braced herself for the worst when she'd sought him out, preparing for anything from cold dismissal to ireful rejection. But how could she have predicted the events that had dominoed since she'd laid eyes on him, knocking sense and good intentions out of reach until she'd found herself wrapped around him, unaware and uncaring if the world was watching, begging for him to possess her, all but offering him carte blanche with her life?

She'd been certain of what he felt. She'd thought they'd

shared something that transcended time and explanations, something real on the most fundamental level.

It had all been an illusion. He'd lied when he'd said he didn't care about labels. He must have been trying to stimulate his glutted senses by leading on yet another desperate female to see how far she'd go, how much of herself she'd offer.

She'd offered him everything. Her pain and shame and trust. She'd left herself wide open, and the blow had crushed her.

In her mind, the feverish moments played again, filled with the cherishment and pleasure his every word and touch had bestowed. Then he'd demanded her name and she'd given it, delighted to complete his knowledge of her, unable to wait to hear it on his lips in all the ways he'd promised.

More images and sensations rose until she felt she was drowning in black ink. Durante, his body losing its gentle ferocity, stiffening, withdrawing, pushing her away.

For one moment, panic had flashed, fear that he, too, got his kicks abusing women. Worse, that something was wrong with her, like Ed had told her, something that drove otherwise normal men to abuse her.

The fear had passed as soon as it had flared. Not Durante. She wouldn't let Ed's vicious psychological sabotage fester again, not for a second. The only one who had something wrong with him was Ed.

But then, something worse than physical abuse had filled Durante's eyes, twisted his face. The rage and revulsion he'd transmitted would leave a deeper scar than anything Ed had done.

After all they'd shared, she hadn't warranted the benefit of a moment's hesitation before he believed the labels she'd been stuck with rather than the reality of her. His decision had been instantaneous, the change in him clearly irreversible. It was the final proof that there was no use. That Ed had won.

He'd been winning for years now, he and his lackeys painting her so black that no one would believe her even if she broke her pact of silence and told the world what a sick bastard he was. And she hadn't cared. She hadn't cared for anyone enough to care what they thought of her. Until Durante…

Was this how despair took root in someone's psyche? Would it now blossom into a monstrous growth that would suffocate everything in its path? Had an injury like this been the origin of her father's suffering? His mother's? Would she react the same way, follow in their footsteps down that bottomless spiral…?

She came to no conclusion before the blackness of exhaustion and heartache dragged her under.

Six

Durante was standing in the distance. His eyes were heavy with disparagement, accusation, his fists clenched at his sides.

She began to walk toward him, her steps gaining speed until she was running. She had to beg him to hear her out. She wasn't what the rumors made her out to be. He of all people knew that. He was the only one she'd shown her real self.

But as she approached him, he turned around and strode away. And she went mad.

She felt her feet lifting off the ground as she caught up with him, sank her fingers in his arm, wrenched. He turned on her with a snarl. And she punched him. In the face. Felt the crunch of cartilage and bones in her hand and his nose, the pain explode through her joints.

She stared up at him in horror as his eyes brimmed with icy rage, and she knew he wouldn't hit back. She almost wished he would, to show her some reaction besides that chilling disdain.

He gave her nothing, stared down at her as if at a maggot.

*Her thoughts were swerving from insisting on paying for the reconstructive surgery that would repair the nose she'd pulverized, to deciding to give him a matching broken jaw to go with it...*when she lurched awake.

Her eyes wouldn't open. She'd cried them shut.

Damn. Damn, damn, damn. Damn him and damn everyone else in this damn stupid world. But the biggest damns were reserved for herself and her stupidity.

She was done being stupid. She'd start by never again shedding a tear. Certainly not over Prince Durante D'Agostino.

She spilled from the bed, barely saw herself in the mirror through her turgid lids as she plodded to her bathroom.

She came out an hour later feeling as if the hot bath had homogenized the pain clamping her chest and melted it to seep through her. She now ached down to her toenails.

She called Megan, her PA, and told her she was taking a few days off. She was sick.

She wasn't lying. She was. Sick of the whole world. Heartache should be at the forefront of ailments one should take sick leave for. And she was taking it.

She needed time to rearrange her mental and emotional papers, invent some priorities, locate her vanished purpose. First on the agenda was purging her memory of Prince Durante D'Agostino.

To do that, she had to admit she owed him a debt of gratitude. He'd made all the slander she'd ever suffered come crashing down on her. She could now face her fury and bitterness, deal with it, put it in perspective and move on.

She should also thank him for curing her of a delusion she'd been suffering from without even realizing it—that miracles happened sometimes and Prince Charming existed somewhere.

Now that she knew for certain that was a load of crap, she could at last have her mind functioning at capacity, unhindered by the insidious virus of such self-sabotaging illusions.

Maybe now she could get rid of all the shackles that had been holding her back. Maybe now she would start to live for real.

Gabrielle looked at her cell phone.

Come on. Do it.

She'd put it off long enough. It had been ten days. She had to call him now. He wouldn't be happy. But he, too, had to face facts. Like she had.

Facts said she'd back down if she waited another moment.

Do. It. Now. She hit the speed dial button, flinching as if she'd hit a remote for a nearby bomb.

The ringing blared on speaker mode until the line disconnected. Relief that he hadn't answered and reluctance to try again sent nausea bubbling in her stomach. *Coward. Do it. Get it over with.*

She pressed the button just as the phone came alive.

She almost dropped it in fright. Then she remembered. She had it on vibration-mode. The caller ID blazed on the screen. The king.

She gulped and hit the answer button.

His voice flowed into her ear, sounding worse than she'd last heard it. "*Figlia mia*, apologies for the delay in answering."

"I should have called much sooner. I-I…" The words congealed into a lump, choked her. *Just spit them out.* "I-it's about your son. I-I tried and failed. He wouldn't talk to me."

That last bit wasn't exactly the truth, but it was true. All the talking Durante had done had been with his "*bella misteriosa.*" He hadn't given *her* the consideration of one word.

Not that the king who'd told her to do "anything" would take her failure lying down. She braced herself for his arguments, for the brunt of his desperation, the distress of having to disappoint it. Just as she thought she was ready for anything, his exhalation almost deflated her with its dejection.

"It was a desperate gamble, Gaby. I was deluded to hope that Durante would relent. Castaldini and I will have to face our fate without his intervention. Forgive me if I caused you any discomfort by involving you in this."

A long time later, she didn't remember what she'd stammered in answer to King Benedetto's apology and acceptance of defeat.

She knew only that her temperature was rising geometrically.

Durante. That cruel, intractable, holier-than-thou bastard.

So he'd condemned her and walked away without a glance back. Fine. She was no one to him. But she was damned if she'd let him get away with doing the same to his father and live happily ever after with his sanctimonious "disconnection."

She didn't care that he thought his position validated. It was still indefensible. And besides, she'd bet he had as much proof of his father's so-called crimes against his mother as he had of *her* alleged ones against male-kind.

She didn't care about the level of demeaning disdain with which he'd no doubt smear her. She was not letting this end without stripping off a few layers of his rhino hide. Maybe she'd even find something beneath to shame into coming through for his father and his kingdom.

She unclasped her death grip on her phone, hit another speed dial button. Megan answered on the first ring.

She fired away. "Megan, I want you to get me every shred of info on Prince Durante D'Agostino of Castaldini. And I don't mean financial and personal profiles. At least, nothing reported in 'reliable' or 'respected' sources. Dig me up all the dirt. Make it thick, and make it quick. I need it…ten days ago."

Durante stared at the wall across his extensive bedroom.

It looked so…tempting. All walls did. He wanted to bang his head against each and every one.

It was the conviction that some explosive pain and serious self-abuse might dampen the volcano seething inside him that tempted him.

How? How had he found himself in this position?

He trusted his instincts, which had steered him through his meteoric rise. But he'd always deferred acting on them until he'd deliberated all ramifications. Instinct didn't equate with impulse to him. He'd believed that he was without urges, did nothing with spontaneity. His closest people told him he took premeditation to uncharted and aggravating heights. That was, until Gabrielle Williamson. *Her.*

His instincts hadn't just totally misled him about her nature. He hadn't thought *once* before accepting their verdict, hadn't found ramifications to ponder as he let himself be swept away in the tide of what he'd thought mutual perfection. She'd satisfied his every demanding taste, his merciless critical eye finding only things to appreciate in her. Even the qualities that she'd put forward as her shortcomings, her hang-ups, had charmed him, secured his unquestioning empathy. And it had all been the practiced routine of a hardened seductress who got ahead in the world by seducing powerful fools like him.

If that night had been her first approach, if he hadn't researched her in advance, if he'd found out her truth after he'd tasted her for real, he wouldn't have been able to walk away, would have blinded himself to wallow in the pleasures she offered. He would have signed that contract, and maybe, like her previous victims, would have ended up signing over half his fortune. Or all of it.

And the worst part? His condition seemed hopeless.

He'd known how hopeless it was when his cousin Eduardo had passed by to check on him with that outspoken bride of his, Jade.

Durante hadn't exited his penthouse for five days, spending that time prowling the cage of his mind. He'd thought it might save his sanity to have a distraction, especially that of people whose show of caring wasn't a setup. So he'd invited them in.

It hadn't played out that way. He'd bristled at their alarm at the sight of him. But when their solicitude had taken the form of questions, prodding, advice, with Giancarlo joining in the chorus of concern, he'd gone off like a landmine.

They'd exchanged the same look that he'd seen on employees faces during the last and most aggressive of his uncharacteristic blowups at his offices. Eduardo and Jade had given Giancarlo—the keeper of the beast—sympathetic murmurs, before they'd left, telling Durante he needed to seek one of two things. A radical lifestyle change. Or psychiatric help. He'd faced it then.

The one thing he needed to seek was her. Gabrielle.

No matter how much he'd told himself to forget her, to move on, he couldn't.

He still couldn't bring himself to seek her out. He missed the persona she'd projected as much as he missed his mother, with the same hopelessness of ever seeing her again. To him, that persona had also disintegrated before it died. The night he'd shared with Gabrielle was entrenched in his memories and senses. He couldn't bear to see her wear another face.

But he'd reached the point where he no longer cared. He had to see her, with any face, at any cost.

He grimaced at his reflection in the full-length mirror then exited his bedroom. At least he no longer looked like the missing link between primates and Neanderthals.

He'd go to her now. This time, he knew what he was getting into, who he was dealing with. He'd walk into the situation with all the brutal clarity of disenchantment, take from her what he needed to get her off his mind and out of his system before walking away…

"I hope this won't get me tossed from the veranda."

Durante rounded on Giancarlo. "If you're worried, as you should be, wear a parachute first. We're high up enough that there's a fifty-fifty chance you'd land with only minor fractures."

Giancarlo grinned. He was Durante's deceased valet's youngest son and was eight years Durante's junior. But for the past seven years, since he'd taken over his father's position, he'd become even more invaluable than his father had been. He was an irreplaceable assistant who observed their situations impeccably in public and in private became a friend as trusted as Durante's younger cousin Eduardo and younger brother Paolo, if less intrusive than either. Not that that said much, because those two were incorrigible. Each had married the "love of his life," and things had gone from bad to dismal.

But Durante wasn't in any condition to humor even Giancarlo. Now that he'd decided to see Gabrielle, he felt as if there were burning coals beneath his feet.

"I know you forbade me to interrupt you unless there was a lot of blood involved—"

"And you're not bleeding," Durante growled. "Yet."

Giancarlo went on as if he hadn't spoken, unperturbed. "—but there's a lady downstairs asking to speak with you. She's—"

"Gabrielle." Her name blared in his mind. He growled it, not wanting Giancarlo to utter it as if he had to be told she was here. When he knew. *Knew.* "Gabrielle Williamson."

Giancarlo nodded. "That's her name, yes. I took the liberty of admitting her to the foyer. I judged she warranted the courtesy, because she was the first woman you ever took to *Angelica,* and the first—and I trust, the last—creature you'll ever sing to. But because you've been like a tiger with a half-ripped-out claw since you stormed down from her residence, I assume you don't want to see her? Shall I tell her you're busy having a breakdown?"

Durante's hiss could have scraped steel. "Bring her up."

Giancarlo gave him an opaque glance. *"Molto bene, principe."*

Durante paced on those coals, feeling the burn spreading through his system. Gabrielle. Here. She'd sought him out. At the exact moment he'd been about to seek her. How did she know that he was ripe for another incursion? How could she be so attuned to thoughts and decisions that seemed random even to him?

Giancarlo returned within two minutes. He wasn't doing a

good job of hiding his smile. Durante would bet he wasn't even trying.

The man cleared his throat as if he were going to sing. "*Signora* Williamson insisted I deliver her message word for word. She said, quote, 'I'm not coming up. You're the one who's coming the hell down here and facing me like a man. If you are one, that is'…unquote."

Durante came the hell down.

After a moment of being unable to believe anyone could not only talk to him that way, but have the temerity to deliver a slap through his right-hand man, to even win said man to her side so that Giancarlo had felt justified and satisfied to transmit it full force.

So he came the hell down. He hurtled, streaked, zoomed and tore his way the hell down. He forced himself to slow once he exited his private elevator. She might have thrown down the gauntlet, but damn if he would give her proof of how she had seeped into his blood, had taken hold of his reactions.

He came to a stop just outside the foyer, depleting reserves of control that he saved for navigating crises of global scope. He yelled inwardly at his instincts, wrestled some rhythm into his heartbeat and breathing. He should make her wait.

He couldn't wait. Her challenge, his eagerness to see her again, was boiling in his blood.

He started walking again, his gait a study in subterfuge, radiating the opposite of what roiled inside him.

He turned the corner and…there she was. Standing at the reception desk, part of her profile visible to him.

She was wearing a skirt suit in another shade of blue, a cross between royal and navy, the richness and depth of the color setting off the clarity of her complexion, the vivid gloss of her hair. The getup was impossibly more flattering than that evening outfit he'd thought the best showcase of her lushness. It molded to her lithe frame, emphasizing her height, the perfection of her proportions, detailing each curve and dip, showing off the symmetry and sculpted creaminess of her legs. Those *legs*. Her flowing skirt had deprived him of seeing them before. He'd had them wrapped around him when he'd been stupid enough to walk away from the promise of fulfillment they'd been offering, almost dealing his potency an irreparable blow.

She was carrying a briefcase. Navy blue to go with her outfit. She looked all business today. And there was this…royal assurance to her bearing, a bring-it-on air to her stance, befitting the potent woman that she was and the mission that had brought her here. To conquer him? He'd bet that was it.

She turned, as if she'd sensed his entrance. She couldn't have possibly seen him, not at the periphery of her vision, not in any reflection. He was still too far for his footsteps to be heard. She had *sensed* him.

And he sensed *her*. Her emanations were unchanged. How did she do that? How did she mess with his perception so that he felt only what she wanted him to feel?

He didn't care. He had to get closer, get more.

He struggled to keep his stride tranquil, as if reaching her was low on his priorities.

When he was finally within arm's reach, he stopped. Her face was a mask captured in blankness, her vibe transmitting nothing of her mood or intentions.

A crack exploded by his ear, on the side of his face, slashing the tranquility of the exclusive foyer's silent occupants and sourceless music.

Seven

Durante blinked, gaped. Beyond stunned. Paralyzed.

He would later swear that she hadn't even moved. But the evidence that she had would resound inside his head forever. Echoes ricocheted off every sound-reflecting surface in the all-marble, chrome and quartz massive space. He barely heard the gasps that went off in a chain reaction of incredulity around him, the quickening footsteps of the guards whose perpetual orders were to stay out of sight.

He made an adamant gesture, banishing them back where they came from. He couldn't bear for others to exist in this moment. Only Gabrielle. Gabrielle, whose eyes were panning away from his with the same void filling them as if she didn't even see him.

Then she brushed past him, walked away with all the grace and serenity of a fairy creature.

It was only when she exited the door the stunned bellman held open for her that Durante registered the burn spreading through his flesh. His hand went instinctively to the pain from the imprint of her fingers, as if to investigate the damage. He moved his mouth from side to side. His jaw felt almost loose.

It excited the hell out of him.

Which made him even more of a colossal fool than he'd realized.

She was pulling his strings. He knew it. But he could sooner resist the pull of a black hole. He rushed out after her.

He caught up with her in less than a minute, her head start and brisk stride no match for his longer legs and urgency.

She suddenly stopped. He overshot her by six strides and retraced them at once.

"Here's the other cheek." He presented her with it. "Go ahead, I know you want to."

She gave no indication that she heard him or even felt him there. She put her briefcase on the ground, opened it, produced a dossier, took papers out, straightened, started reading.

"Prince Durante Benedetto D'Agostino. Eldest son of the King of Castaldini, and therefore, according to the ancient laws of succession, the only member of the extensive D'Agostino royal family ineligible for the crown."

She was reading him a report? On him?

"To prove to the world that his inability to run for the crown meant nothing to him, Prince Durante decided to be king of his own kingdom, emperor of his own empire."

Would there be a point to this somewhere? Knowing what he did about her, she was bound to have a whopper. But what could it be?

"During his meteoric ascent from age twenty, the prince masterminded takeovers that redefined the word *hostile*. Those he took an ax to say that they would have preferred it if he'd taken a contract on their lives and been done with it. Two of those he destroyed *did* end up taking their own lives. Then, at thirty-five, he engineered a market crash that sent thousands into bankruptcy while catapulting himself from mere billionaire status to that of financial god. Ever since, he's been shearing his way through the pantheon, cutting down fellow deities in his climb to the absolute and solitary top."

He'd heard all that before. Not that articulate or concentrated, and certainly not to his face.

She wasn't finished. "On a personal level, it is said that Prince Durante is as cold-blooded and unrepentant a lady-killer as he is a rival-slayer. He is known to pick beauties from those who crowd around his feet, use them and discard them. On one notable occasion, one of his fleeting indulgences tried to commit suicide and is still undergoing intensive psychiatric treatment. Her family reports that Prince Durante systematically destroyed her self-esteem, and she ended up despising herself. A second woman—a married one—said that Prince Durante's influence rivals that of the Prince of Darkness himself. After her husband divorced her and gained custody of their two toddlers, denying her even visitation rights, the spellbound and discarded woman still said that, even knowing where it would lead, she'd do it again. She only wished Prince Durante would take her back."

And he got her point. Right through the heart.

Something else skewered him there. Shame.

He of all people, who suffered slander, shouldn't have been party to perpetuating it, to judging her and carrying out his judgment based on secondhand information.

But beyond shame, which was self-indulgent and worthless, something harsher tore at him. The hurt he felt emanating from her.

He could no longer deny it. His instincts hadn't been tampered with. They'd told him the truth all along. Everything *else* had lied. Everything he'd heard about her had been as false as the reports propagated against him by his enemies.

The fair reports were also out there, as abundant, but they

weren't as interesting as the defamatory ones, weren't sensational enough to be bandied around. His friends didn't feel the need to defend him and he'd never wanted them to, leaving the field wide open to the foes who spoke loudest, were most persistent.

She stopped sifting through the pages. "All reports of Prince Durante's atrocities remain unsubstantiated allegations, because he manages to remain beyond reproach, faultlessly covering his amoral and immoral tracks. As such, he is considered to be our era's only Machiavellian prince. Some even claim that he used Machiavelli's most famous work, *Il Principe—The Prince*—the immortal guide to acquiring and maintaining power, as the template from which he forged his persona and kingdom. What he added of his own heartlessness and intelligence has created a modern hybrid even the philosopher couldn't have imagined being spawned."

He raised his hands, surrendering. "*Abbastanza,* Gabrielle. Enough. You can stop now. I get it."

Without a glance at him, she rearranged the papers back into the dossier, bent to pick up her briefcase. He caught her arm.

"We need to talk." Her blank stare deepened his desperation. He gritted his teeth. "*I* need to talk."

"That you do, now, is of no consequence. I am not here to talk. I am here to tell you something. You're a paranoid bastard who's so full of your own convictions and hang-ups, you can't see how your actions injure and maim people around you. If you have one shred of humanity—and according to your lofty opinion of yourself, you're full of…it—I'm giving you an assignment to find out how much you *do* possess. Write down a list of all the people in your life. Be honest about their condition today, emotionally, psychologically, financially, and calculate the role your condemning, unforgiving nature has played in it."

Her accusation slid right off him. Not because it didn't shame him that it might be true, but because his only concern was for undoing the injury he'd caused *her.*

Pedestrians and even drivers were slowing down to watch the scene unfolding between their city's most famous resident royal and the stunning woman who was clearly telling him off. Some were openly gawking. Some were clicking away on their cell phones.

Not that he cared. But he was beginning to realize the role speculation and the media must have played in smearing her reputation.

He had to take her away from prying eyes and wagging tongues. "Come up with me, Gabrielle. Please."

"No." She extricated her arm from his urgent grip. "If there's one thing I've learned from my...vast experience, it's what to avoid in the interest of self-preservation. I thought being punched black and blue was the worst thing that had happened to me, but now I know how hard *you* hit, I'd be crazy if I came near you again. Goodbye, Prince Durante."

He blocked her path. "*Per favore,* Gabrielle, you must listen to me."

Her disdain would have annihilated a lesser man. At least a less determined one. "As you listened to me? Oh, wait, you didn't give me the chance to say anything to listen to. You heard my name, recalled the report some bored assistant collated on me and disregarded everything you learned about me during that night you kept calling magical and unprecedented—the line you handed me when you wanted to score another one-night stand. Funny part is, although your criteria for one-nighters are reportedly pretty flexible, it seems you draw the line somewhere. At my level."

He surged forward as if to stem the flow of her bitterness. She took two steps back to his every step forward in a wretched parody of a waltz.

He stopped, clenched his fists so he wouldn't haul her over his shoulder and take her someplace where he could make her listen. "You think I leave functions I sponsor, dedicate whole nights and ignore work—for days on end—for anything, let alone what you make sound like scratching an itch? It *was* all real and magical to me."

Something terrible flared in her eyes, which turned the color of turbulent smoke. "Yet as soon as you heard my name, you looked at me as if I were something vile. You made me feel soiled, worthless, like no one has ever made me feel—not the sick jerk I married, not the paparazzi who scoop up his poison to mix with their own and peddle it to the rumor addicts of the world."

Suddenly a man with a cell phone held up toward them came too close. The bastard wanted to get sound with his footage.

"Gabrielle, let's stop this sideshow. Come inside with me."

"This *sideshow* will stop when you move out of my way so I can get on mine. So move. Just don't forget to make that list. Start with your father and work your way down."

"I will. I promise. But I'll start with you."

"Don't bother. I'm sure you felt validated as you walked away from me. Enjoy the company of your prejudice, Prince Durante."

"*Maledizione,* Gabrielle, I wasn't feeling validated when I walked away, I was feeling violated. I've been incapacitated ever since. All the vile things I had heard about you overwhelmed me until all I could see was another trap like those that have been laid for me ever since I became old enough for women to consider me a ticket to wealth and social status. But I'm used to those traps. I watch them being laid in bored amusement. When I thought I'd failed to see yours, I was enraged. But what really hurt was when I started negotiating with myself to let you have whatever you want, so that I could have you, too. That was the lowest place I've ever been. So I walked away."

Her eyes darkened to the color of cumulus about to hurtle down a deluge. Then she gave a slow nod. "Okay. It must be tough being you. It must be almost impossible for you to trust people's motivations enough to indulge in even healthy casual contact. I can relate to that, because the would-be exploiters in my own life make it tough for me to trust anyone. In your case, that must be multiplied by a factor of thousands. I just hope you remember it wasn't my idea to hide my identity that long, that I only delayed introducing myself until you gave me a fair hearing, fearing the reaction you ended up so predictably having anyway."

"You don't have to remind me how things went, or that it was I who steered the situation. I remember every second of that night."

"I'm sure you had fun superimposing your version of my 'trap laying' on every second."

"Fun? I said I was paralyzed for the past few days. I've been going mad wondering how you fooled my instincts so totally, yet wanting you so fiercely still, I was willing to risk anything to have you."

"Sure. You were so out of your mind you would have never seen me again if I hadn't insulted you into confronting me."

"I wasn't in the least insulted. I was stunned, then thrilled. And I was on my way to find you when you arrived."

That startled her. But not for long. She clearly discounted his claim, huffed. "What a coincidence, huh?"

"I don't believe it's a coincidence. I think we're attuned to one another on a very basic level. We reached the same decision, reached our limit for staying apart at the same time."

"Not exactly the same time. I arrived here when the idea of coming after me was still in the embryonic stage with you."

His lips twitched. "Actually, it was in the last stage of labor."

Her lips almost gave in to the humor tugging at them. Almost. He knew part of her was reveling in their volley match, but she wasn't about to let him get off that easy. As she shouldn't.

"Still, according to your theory, because I acted first on that transmission between us, either my receptors are keener, or signals take longer to penetrate that thick skull of yours."

This was a serious situation. As serious as when she'd been relating her life story. She'd poked fun then, too, if at herself.

He shouldn't. He couldn't help it.

He threw back his thick skull and laughed.

No one else had or would ever talk to him like that. Only her.

He stopped laughing abruptly when her gaze strayed behind him. He turned. His bodyguards had closed in and were trying and failing to look as if they were not on full alert.

"So even your bodyguards are terrified I might suck you dry or swallow you whole, huh?" She smirked.

"Should you really be saying things like 'suck you dry' and 'swallow you whole' to me, out here, where I can't do much about it? Now that's a spectacularly effective method of punishment."

Divine color cascaded from her sculpted cheekbones to flood her face and neck. His mouth tingled to latch onto every inch until *he* swallowed *her* whole.

"You turn everything into a sexual innuendo," she muttered.

"Believe it or not—and you're not in the mood to believe anything I say—I never did before. I never saw the attraction in the practice. Now I can't see anything but."

She fidgeted, as if her skin were suddenly too tight. No matter how affronted, how hurt she was, her body still yearned for his. That was the one thing he hadn't doubted. He'd thought she'd been playing him, but enjoying him with every fiber of her voluptuous body while at it.

She stole a self-conscious look at his bodyguards. "They're almost reaching for their guns. Do you have an APB out on imminent redheaded danger?"

"They're jumpy because the last time I stopped in the street to talk to someone I know, he stabbed me." Horror burst into her eyes. After a frozen moment, they wrenched from his, careened down his body, as if she could see the injury through his clothes. "Then he bid ten million for a chance to say he was sorry."

"He was the…? Oh, God…was it…? Are you…?" She seemed unable to go on, her throat working as if swallowing tears.

After what he'd done to her, seeing her so disturbed to think of him hurt was too much.

He interrupted her agitation. "I moved out of the direct path of his thrust. He only penetrated skin and muscles in my left flank."

Her hand jerked up, trembled as it reached halfway to where his injury was, before she fisted it, pulled it back.

The unwilling gesture of concern closed his throat. "And you know what? I'll add him to my list. I was adamant about not giving him a second chance, but now I'll seek him out to talk this through. I find I have a new wealth of empathy for him and his need for forgiveness now that I'm in the same position."

She gaped. "You're equating a physical wound with a moral one?"

"I think the moral one is far worse in this situation. I didn't lose any sleep over the flesh wound. And there are no lingering ill effects. But even though I don't expect you to forgive me any more easily than I chose to forgive him, I demand that you give me another chance, so that I can earn your forgiveness."

"Demand? My, is that a royal edict, Your Highness?"

His lips twisted. "I'm a bit out of my jurisdiction, royally speaking. But then, this is my new kingdom, as your report put it. My demands here *are* considered edicts."

She coughed a furious chuckle. "You've just shot through the barrier of unbelievability into the realm of what's-he-on." She thrust her dossier at him. "Here, keep this. Read it through for laughs if you want to see how creative people can get in their vindictiveness, in case you don't fully know yet. I only read you the highlights, which amounted to three pages out of sixty-two."

She walked away then. He knew she wasn't going to stop.

He had to get her back anyway he could. He called after her.

"You wanted me to write a book baring the details of my life and journey to success, the workings of my mind and methods. I'm interested."

She whirled around, a magnificent lioness with a mane of fire, her eyes iridescent with ire. "Oh, no, you're not."

Lust corkscrewed in his loins. He savored the twisting ache, cocked his head. "You've changed your mind about your offer?"

Her eyes narrowed at him. "You know I haven't."

"How do I know that when you didn't bring it up again?"

"I didn't bring it up at all. First you wouldn't hear of business, then you wouldn't hear anything I had to say."

"I want to hear everything you have to say now."

"*Sei serio?* You're serious? This isn't just pretext for…for…"

"For taking you to bed? No. Although I am suffering permanent damage here as we speak, because I haven't taken you to bed and kept you there for the last ten days, because I'm standing in the middle of smog-infested, ground-level downtown New York instead of lying inside you in a bed eighty floors up in serenity and seclusion, I *am* interested in hearing about your book offer."

Suspicion flared higher in her eyes. "And why are you?"

"Because I believe that anything you propose will have a lot to recommend it. I didn't say I'd accept, though."

She pursed her lips. "Fair enough. I want you to accept only if I convince you, not because you want me in your bed. In fact, I won't sign a thing if that's your motive. Contrary to 'common knowledge,' I don't barter my body for business deals."

"I don't either." She narrowed her eyes. He held out his hand, inviting, placating, coaxing, barely holding back the need to reestablish the connection, to drag her into his arms. "I owe you one hour of the exclusive use of my ear. Then, if you wish, you can have the exclusive use of the rest of my body."

Eight

Gabrielle looked up at Durante from his kitchen table.

He was handing her a hot chocolate he'd prepared himself.

She took the very masculine, clean-cut, but clearly expensive and possibly specially made fine China mug from him. He brought his own and sat across from her, dominating his stainless steel and obsidian marble spaceship of a kitchen.

This was surreal. To be in his kitchen of all places, with him waiting on her. In fact, she didn't know if she'd actually walked back to his building, crossed the extensive foyer littered with still-gaping denizens, entered his private elevator and ended up in his floor-wide penthouse, or if he'd levitated her there.

She wouldn't put it past him. Those reports hadn't exaggerated his influence at all.

He leaned across the table, enveloped her hand in his—the one that had slapped him—smoothed his thumb over her knuckles, before turning it over and doing the same to her palm.

"Can you please stop that?"

"Why? You like it. From your breathing, I'd say too much. Is that the problem?"

"I didn't come here with slapping you in mind, Durante..."

"But you saw me and emotion overwhelmed your judgment?"

"Quite the reverse actually. I held myself back at the last moment." She told him what she'd done in her dream.

He bellowed with laughter. "So I owe it to your self-mastery that I'm not now undergoing rhinoplasty and a jaw reset." He wiped tears of hilarity with one hand, the other taking hers to his lips. He planted tiny kisses on knuckle after another, zapping her with enough voltage to power a block. "Ah, *Gabriella mia, grazie a Dio* you held back, or these works of divine art would be bruised and swollen now. But let me assure you, your slap almost achieved one of your wishes. My jaw may never resume its former position."

"If the way you're using your mouth is any indication, I'd say I made it extra efficient."

He lunged across the table. Before she even blinked, he twisted hair at her nape, tilted up her face and claimed her lips in a compulsive kiss. He inhaled as he took and took of her until she felt he'd drawn her essence inside him. The warm, moist firmness of his lips, the way they plucked at hers, massaged, kneaded, shot tremors from her lips to her core. Then he exhaled and thrust deep, flooding her with his taste and scent.

Each kiss he gave her was new, different, giving her more and more. It was as if, through every press and glide and thrust, he was fathoming her preferences, many she didn't know herself, deciphering the code of her responses, the combination to unlock the pleasure her body had the potential to feel and never had.

She'd become addicted from the first exposure, had felt hollow knowing she'd never have more.

She did now. Could have far more if she dared. Again.

His rejection still reverberated in her marrow.

She recoiled from the echo of anguish just as he released her, sat down heavily in his chair, threw his head back and closed his eyes, veins standing out in his corded neck.

He let out a slow, ragged breath and opened his eyes. Streaks of brilliant blue radiation seemed to sweep over her and through her with unbridled carnality. "In the interest of self-preservation, let's drink our concoction and discuss your offer." He sat forward, linked his hands. "So, what makes your offer different? You advertized your certainty that I couldn't refuse it."

She blinked. "I only said that to Gerald Whittacker as he wanted to champion my request but wanted to make sure I was on to something that wouldn't be a waste of your time. I didn't think he'd relay it to you."

"How do you know Gerald?"

She set her teeth. "How do you think?"

He sighed. "I admit, I thought…the worst. At first." She bristled, and his eyes gentled. "Now I'm just curious, not suspicious."

She searched his face. There was no trace of the distrust and condemnation that had destroyed her the day he'd walked away.

Something inside her broke down in relieved sobs.

She bit her lip on the surge of moronic elation. "He used to be Dad's golf instructor before my dad's condition worsened, and before Gerald made his fortune. I earned myself a soft spot in his heart by running my own heart out retrieving balls for him."

He closed his eyes, tipped his head and smiled, as if he were watching something funny and endearing across his lids. When he opened his eyes, they were filled with something far more dangerous than passion, suspicion or anger. Tenderness.

"You must have been younger than five. I can just imagine you, strong limbs and boundless energy, streaking after errant balls, in pursuit of approval and smiles."

That was how it had been exactly. Gerald had given her a glimpse of what paternal indulgence could be like, when her father hadn't been able to provide it. And somehow Durante had looked back in time and knew. She wanted him to know the rest.

"While I'm debunking the myths about my being a gold-digging man-eater, I want you to know where they came from."

His wave was dismissing, adamant. "I don't need explanations."

"*I* need to tell you. The details, anyway. I already told you the basics…about my ex. I've never told anybody the truth. In fact, that secrecy is the reason behind my negative reputation. You see, I didn't bring up my hospital stay and the charges I pressed during divorce proceedings. My lawyers insisted that if I exposed him, he'd be harmed, but I'd gain nothing but more lawsuits and having him in my life endlessly. They got me a huge settlement in return for silence. It wasn't enough punishment for what he did to me, but I figured I was cutting that monster in half. But then, he took advantage of my silence to defame me. He gets more vicious as time goes by, knowing that if I speak up now, I'll be known as the bitch who's slandering the poor ex she robbed of half his fortune. That final day in court, he swore he'd make my life hell. And he sure is trying his worst. I guess the few men I rejected afterward make a good chorus for his venom."

His look had darkened as she spoke, was almost black now.

She groaned. "What are you thinking?"

Something chilling slithered in the depths of his eyes. His lips spread in a frightening parody of a smile. He looked like some malevolent deity. She already knew he was formidable, but she could now see how deadly he could be.

"I'm thinking it's time Edward Jamieson lost the other half of his fortune. And for the truth about him to become public. A man like him would be a serial abuser. There are bound to be other women he's hurt and paid off into silence. I'm also thinking it's time for his first wife's death to be fully investigated."

She gaped at him. "Remind me never to become your enemy."

His switch from ferocity to fondness was dizzying. "Not only is there no danger of that, but I'm only an effective enemy to those who've been their own worst enemies. All I need to do to crush him is expose the crimes he committed."

"So that's how you decimate your rivals, huh? Through their own wrongdoing?"

"And by doing nothing wrong myself, so no one can retaliate. Except with allegations such as what you came armed with today."

She chewed her lip. "I would have told you to leave him alone, that he and his lies don't matter, if you hadn't reminded me that he could be abusing other women—women who may not be able to defend themselves like I did. So, as long as the investigations are honest, by all means, crush away."

He crooked her a whimsical smile. "As long as? You think there's a chance I'd fabricate evidence? Frame him?"

"No! I know from your history—and from personal experience—that you retaliate with disproportionate force when crossed, but I've come to believe that you do so when you think you're justified, not out of malice. I believe you're unforgiving, but not unscrupulous. You're an avenger—you might act before you get your facts straight, but you're never a villain."

He sat forward, placed both elbows on the quartz table, cupped his face in his palms, his eyes heavy with exhilaration and indulgence. "That's quite a testimony. I think." He winked at her. "If I ever run for public office anywhere, my slogan will be An avenger, never a villain."

She was struggling to convince her heart to restart when he drawled, "So...sell me on your proposal."

Thankful for the detour away from personal landmines, she breathed deep, struggled to access the pitch she'd prepared.

"Okay." She sat forward. "The book I envision is not like any you've received offers to write. I'm not after the sensational angles in your life, real or fabricated. In fact, I don't want you to expose anything about your personal life beyond your health, exercise and relaxation habits. You know, anything that kept you functioning to capacity for the past twenty years, soaring from one pinnacle to the next. I want you to explore your drive, your discipline. I want this to be the work-ethic motivation book of all time, a book any young person would read and be inspired to jump up and tackle the world."

His eyes had grown serious as she talked. He suddenly huffed. "It's ironic to hear you saying 'soaring' when those closest to me are insisting I'm perilously close to crashing and burning."

Her heart skipped another beat. "What's *your* opinion?"

"I think they're on to something. At least, they *were*."

The meaning simmering in his eyes quivered in her heart. She almost shouted for him to stop. Keep it strictly sexual. She might know how to handle it if he did. But he didn't, and she couldn't hope he meant what she hoped he meant. Therein lay certain annihilation.

But there was something far stronger than fear for her fate. Concern for him. "Do you have any complaints, any symptoms?"

He started to dismiss her question, then changed his mind, leveled his eyes on her. "The main symptom is that I 'retaliate with disproportionate force when crossed.' I never had a temper and it's maddening that I seem to have developed one."

"So what's loosening your screws?"

"Public opinion says I've been chronically fatigued and sleep deprived for years. All I know is that I'm working more and more and sleeping less and less. When I do sleep, I don't remember any of my dreams, to the point that I think I don't dream."

"Do you need to work that hard?"

"That's what my friends keep asking."

Her eyebrows shot up. "You have friends?"

His laugh boomed. "Wonders will never cease, will they? I, for one, sometimes wonder how I do. There are two in partic-ular I want you to meet, my cousin and his bride. I think you'll really get along with Jade. She hones her tongue at the same rapier maker that you do." She made a face at him and he laughed again. "No, I don't have to work a fraction as hard to 'maintain my power.' But I've become unable to slow down, like a train without brakes. It's become self-perpetuating, sort of an addiction. I guess I am too much like my father. He slowed down when he was in his fifties. And he still streaked past everyone else."

It shook her. Again. The enormity of feeling that radiated from him when he mentioned his father. The first time there'd been so much anger it had thrown her. This time there was no doubt. He *loved* him.

It was probably the magnitude of his love that caused his feelings of betrayal to be so vast, made what he believed to be the breach of his trust so irredeemable.

She wanted to protest that he had it all wrong, as he had with her, that he didn't have to live with disillusionment eating away at him, that he had to give his father the benefit of the doubt, even if the king couldn't provide evidence to exonerate himself.

But she couldn't. She'd given King Benedetto her word. And if she started that argument, Durante would notice she wasn't just drawing parallels between his treatment of her and his father, would see her emotional investment in his father's cause. He'd ask. And if he asked, she'd tell him. And she *couldn't*.

But maybe there was some way around this, other than breaking her word. Durante was starting to talk, as she was convinced he hadn't before. Maybe he'd purge his angst, give his father a chance, like he was willing to give one to the man who'd stabbed him. Maybe things would go where the king hoped.

Not that it made her situation any better. When she'd given her word, she'd thought there'd be nothing but business contact with Durante, that she'd be the voice of reason before she exited his life at the conclusion of the deal. Now everything had changed and she felt as if she was lying to him when she—

"Any number of millions for your thoughts."

Durante's deep purr short-circuited her turmoil. She breathed a nervous laugh. "You always toss around carte blanche like that?"

He sipped his drink, his gaze caressing her over his mug's rim. "Never even in jest. Only for you. So where did you go?"

She reached for her mug, gulped the rich sweetness as if it would fortify her. "I was musing if your case is genetic."

He took another sip, looking thoughtful. "Maybe. Probably. Still think I'd make a good example for the youths of the world?"

"I think this glitch in your system…humanizes you, makes your experience more accessible, can make young people aspire to walk in your footsteps while learning how to recognize bad habits before they take hold of their lives."

He gave her a bedeviling smile. "As they did of mine?"

She groaned. "Believe it or not, I used to be a very suave negotiator. But don't hold my big mouth against the project, okay? I do believe your story can change lives, and although I know there is no advance that wouldn't make you yawn, if this is a bestseller—and I can't imagine it won't be—Le Roi will only keep what would float us and the rest goes to charity. All returns will be distributed for free wherever you choose."

He frowned. "You company is in trouble?"

"You didn't know?"

"I ran a personal background check on you. If I'd decided to talk business, I would have run the business check."

So that was why he hadn't brought up her company's Castaldinian connections. He didn't know of them. She might not be able to tell him of her connection with his father, but she had to inform him of those, before he ran that check.

He ran a tender finger down her cheek. "Tell me."

And she told him. Everything. Everything she could.

He'd stilled when she'd mentioned Castaldini, his expression going opaque. When she fell silent, he lowered his eyes, lost in thought. Then he finally looked back at her. His eyes were glittering with wonder.

"So this is why you were interested in me originally."

She gave a difficult nod. It was the truth, but not the whole truth. And she was not at liberty to share the rest.

"This *is* fate, for you to be connected to my homeland, to seek me out, to let me find you through this connection." He rose, came around, pulled her to her feet, his hands filled with such gentleness. Thoughts scattered on his kitchen's porcelain floor as he put a loose arm low around her waist. "But don't worry, about anything. Everything is going to be fine, I promise."

She blinked up at him in confusion as he walked her back through his hangar-sized penthouse. "What do you mean?"

They passed through a twenty-foot-wide arch into a sitting room with one wall made of floor-to-ceiling glass overlooking the most spectacular view of Manhattan and the ocean that she'd ever seen.

"Just what I said." He took her to the wall window, his smile the essence of reassurance. She looked down the eighty-floor sheer drop and pressed back into him. He tugged her a couple of steps back where she could get the full impact of the view without activating any twinges of acrophobia. "Everything will work out."

And that was clearly all she'd get from him on the subject.

She stood there, unable to fracture the moment, break the meld, her body a battleground of desire and dread. Then he whispered against her temple, "I never wrote anything, let alone a book. I was the worst essay writer in my class, in any language. My essays, to borrow an Americanism, sucked. A few dry-as-tinder lines with a sledgehammer of a conclusion along the lines of 'Own your mistakes or you're screwed.'"

She pushed away at last, put much-needed air between them, raised an eyebrow. "As you always do?"

He took her ridicule with a grin. "I try. I'm trying now."

She gave him a considering look. "Hmm. It's clear you owned far more mistakes than not. In your professional life. That's why *that* isn't screwed." He grimaced at her allusion that his personal one was. "Anyway, that sledgehammer would be perfect for the heading of a chapter. That's the kind of succinct conclusion I want you to fill the book with. Coming from you, the epitome of phenomenal success, you have the platform and the credibility to make self-help gurus of the known universe look like they're spouting unsupported nonsense."

"I might have the platform and the credibility, but I also have a handicap to negate them both. I write like you sing."

She burst out giggling. "Trust me, you can't be that bad."

He grinned back at her, riddling her sight with blind spots. "See, another handicap. No subtlety. I was trying and failing to hint that I'll need help." He pulled her to him, his hands filled with careful power as he contained her. "Lots and lots of it."

She moaned. "Durante…"

He lowered his head. "*Sì, Gabriella.* Say my name like that."

She averted her face before his lips connected with hers. It was like leaping over one volcano to plunge into another. His lips scorched down her face instead, her neck, his whispers of her name an invocation, a supplication, tampering with all electrical activity powering her. Her brain waves blipped, her heart rhythm plunged into arrhythmia.

She gasped, pushed at him. He let her go at once, his gaze heavy with desire and regret. "Still punishing me?"

"I don't indulge in pointless posturing. Life's too short."

"Exactly. And this, along with the past ten days, is time we won't get back."

"Philosophy is great, when one can afford it. I can't. Life is also too short to spend any of it feeling as miserable as I did during those ten days."

He reached for her again. "And you won't. I promise."

She scrambled away as if from the ledge of this skyscraper. "I-I came up here for two reasons, Durante. Because I believed you were interested in my offer. And because I couldn't take one more would-be paparazzi covering our little sideshow."

He grunted. "Forget them. They don't matter."

"Really? Strange. You condemned me based on 'facts' people like them perpetuated."

"*Ero uno sciocco*, I was a fool. A moron."

"*And* a senseless jerk. Oh, wait, am I allowed to say 'jerk' to Your Highness? No? Bummer. I'll say it anyway."

"You're allowed to say anything to My Highness as long as you deem to talk to me at all. But senseless jerk that I am, I came to my senses. Don't I get points toward a second chance for that?"

"You would have, if you *had* come to your senses. Which you didn't. I slapped some sense into you. You were wallowing in your senselessness and decided to seek me in spite of what you believed, not because you no longer believed it. You thought I was a succubus but were risking being drained of life to satisfy your curiosity and lust. Or was danger what fueled your desire, sort of like the rush of sticking your hand in a snake pit?"

"I was doing it in spite of the danger I thought you represented, not because of it. I don't get my kicks that way."

"You get them by thinking the worst of people. By never giving them the chance to defend themselves, condemning them and carrying out the sentence. And if one of your victims is your own father, I guess I was in great company."

"*Maledizione*, Gabrielle…*sì, bene?* It's true, only those who matter can make me react emotionally. I've only ever had those crippling feelings in relation to two people in my life. My mother and my father. Now you."

"That's supposed to make me feel special? I got the full, mutilating effect of your anger because of how much I mattered?"

"Hard to believe but…*sì.*"

"What's freaking impossible to believe is you. I live with a lot of casual cruelty, but now I know how it can hurt when someone who *matters* doles it out. I have no support system and the only one who'll defend me is me. The only way I know how to do that is to stay away from you. So if you're not interested in my offer if it doesn't come attached with me in your bed, say so and let me go."

"You said you understood why I reacted the way I did. If you do, then you realize it will never happen again."

"All I know is that you judged me based on unsubstantiated evidence. The evidence against you was as damning, yet I believed my own senses, my own mind, my own experience of you."

He raked his fingers through his hair, linked them at the back of his head in a gesture of a man at a total loss. He closed his eyes, rumbling the unmistakable fury of self-abuse. Then he opened them, all previous lightness and cajoling gone.

"I've broken your trust in my basic fairness, in my ability to always treat you with consideration and respect."

Every muscle in her face trembled. He'd put her biggest fear in words. She nodded. A tear splashed on her lip.

He winced as if the tear had hit his flesh, burned it. "I would offer amends, anything at all, but it seems I hurt you too much and it won't matter what I do, not now." He rubbed a hand over his eyes. "I *was* interested to hear your offer. And you've convinced me. I agree to the basic concept, but we'll work out the specifics. Send me the draft of the contract at your convenience. I'll inform you of any amendments at the earliest."

When he said no more, she stuck her hands at her waist. "So what are you saying? 'You don't want my amends so I won't bother to make them'? And then what? 'Would have been fun knowing you'?"

His eyes probed her. "What are *yóu* saying, Gabrielle?"

"That it's surely heartening to see how long you thought 'making amends' warranted. It's been—" she flicked a look at her watch "—forty-eight minutes. That must be an all-time record for you. Bet you don't even consider apologizing to anyone. Guess that's another thing that makes me mighty special. Yay me."

"Are you being a contrary female, *Gabriella mia?* Saying you want something, then getting disappointed when you get it? Or are you saying no when you mean yes, to make me grovel?"

"Are you being a condescending chauvinist, Your Highness? I was commenting on the limits of your perseverance. When I didn't collapse under your charm after a few nudges…poof. Suddenly it's "I would do anything, but you don't want me to, so I'll save myself the trouble.' Talk about staying power. Lack of, that is."

"Do watch what you say to me right now, *Gabriella mia.* I am in a very critical condition. I'm a breath away from an all-day-and-night campaign to prove my…staying power to you." Desire forked from every point his eyes touched to her womb. He trickled a phantom touch down her cheek. "I was letting you go because I thought you were still raw, that I was causing you more distress. I was giving you a couple of days to cool down— *maledizione,* I probably wouldn't have lasted a couple of hours. Then I was coming after you and never stopping until you gave me a second chance."

"Great. And because *never* has forever scope, you won't mind if I go now. Plenty of time for 'we'll see, won't we' in forever…"

And she was in his arms, singed in the inferno of his ardor. "Don't walk away, *bellissima.* I'm the knee-jerk jerk here."

"Let me go and no one will get hurt, Your Royal Jerkness."

"It's too late. I would have gotten hurt if I'd let you go before I laughed with you, caused your tears, tasted your hunger."

"Durante…" Her voice broke as she put her fear into words. "You're way out of my league."

"You're the only one I want in mine. Say you want me, too."

She squeezed her eyes, shuddered. "You *know* I do."

"Then forgive me, *Gabriella mia.* And don't be afraid, I won't consider this license to forgive myself." She succumbed, nodded, buried her face in his neck. He groaned in relief, branded her forehead in a convulsive kiss. *"Grazie molto, bellissima."*

She burrowed deeper into his neck. This was inevitable. He was inexorable. She craved him with such intensity that she no longer cared if it all ended horribly tomorrow. She had to have now.

"Now tell me…" He swept her up in his arms. "Would you mind if I took you fast and ferocious the first couple of times?"

Nine

"The first couple of times?"

Durante lips spread at the squeak in Gabrielle's voice, the disbelief in her eyes. At having her precious weight and surrender filling his arms after almost losing her, in so many ways.

And he had almost lost her. In the one way he wouldn't have been able to live with. Through his own actions.

She was everything he'd felt she was from the first moment, everything that captured his imagination and commanded his appreciation, roused his soul and aroused his senses. Proud and fierce, sharp and quick, pure of heart, rich in soul, as vulnerable as she was indomitable. He'd read her as accurately as she'd read him. He was certain now. No more doubts. He'd never let the outside world come between them again.

This time, and from now on, there would be no holding back. There'd be only holding on. He'd never let her go.

He gathered her tighter in his arms, filled his eyes and senses with her beauty as she clung to him, answered her incredulity.

"Maybe after the second time I'll be able to slow down a bit. I can guarantee slow, though, so slow until you beg, until you faint with pleasure, after the third time."

"The *third* time?"

"Do you hear an echo?" He smiled into the eyes he could swear were emitting silver heat and hunger and…anxiety?

He wanted to kick himself. With what she'd suffered at a man's hand, she could be totally misinterpreting his words.

He stopped in the massive vestibule separating reception and living quarters. Even though everything in him screamed not to lose contact with her, he gently put her down. She swayed, clung to him, her eyes a mixture of drugged arousal, confusion and alarm.

"What are you thinking, *bellissima?*"

She blinked at him. "Thinking? You think I can think now?"

"You look…anxious." She bit a lip that trembled her confession. He cupped her face, freed that lip with a caressing thumb. "Is there anything you want me to know? Anything you don't want me to do? Anything that might trigger distasteful memories?"

Understanding crept over her face, followed by urgency. "No! No, Durante, don't think that, please. If I'm anxious it's because I don't know if I can…you see, I-I've never…you know…"

Suspicion rose in him at her embarrassment, became certainty in a heartbeat. "You never enjoyed sex."

"I-I know I can, since I-I…"

"You pleasure yourself. But you never climax with a partner."

Her color became dangerous. "Do you know everything? Or are you reading my mind?" She shut her eyes in mortification.

He brushed her eyes open with both thumbs. "And I told you I'll take you fast and ferocious and you thought I'd take my pleasure and leave you feeling used and frustrated."

"No, no…I know you wouldn't…it's me…I'm having…"

His lips twisted. "Performance anxiety."

"You *do* know everything!" She buried her face in her hands, before dropping them, exhaling, eyes downcast. "Way to go, huh? Telling you that now, ruining everything."

"You told someone before, probably your ex, and he used it to blame you for his shortcomings," he growled. Giving that piece of trash a taste of his own medicine was fast becoming an emergency. "And of course he told you how he never failed to please other women, women who miraculously attain orgasm through their own feminine normalcy, even with a fumbling, re-pulsive, self-seeking, two-minute scumbag who thinks all he has to do to be a great lover is get an erection, insert and ejaculate."

She coughed a distressed laugh. "Basically…yeah. Apart from that description of him, which he of course didn't say, but was and did. This is uncanny. How do you know that? Do you know men like that?"

"There *are* no men like that. He's not a man, he's one of a breed of inferiority-ridden, ugliness-infested bastards who feel nothing but the urge to relieve their pathetic itches, who know no higher motivation than to grab, use, and when confronted with their own deficiencies, abuse."

She nodded, averted her eyes. "I agree."

He frowned. She didn't look as if she did, not fully. "But?"

She looked as if she hoped the parquet floor would become an ocean she could plunge into and never resurface. "But in this case, it wasn't his fault alone. I-I tried with others…many others…"

Images charred imprints on his mind. Of her, in other men's beds, her body open to their exploitation, at their mercy…

A wave of nausea rose until it tinged his sight with yellowed bile, something monstrous, grotesque ripping him open from the gut outward, fang and talon.

Jealousy. Something he'd never imagined feeling before.

Next moment, it subsided. It had no soil to take root in. The past meant nothing, not hers, not his. Or hers did only in terms that he must adjust his approach, from the freedom of taking by storm the woman he'd thought experienced, holding nothing back in his certainty that she could match his ferocity, know her preferences and demand them from him, to the care of taking the woman who'd experienced nothing but abuse and dissatisfaction.

"You were a virgin when you married him?" She nodded, her unease bordering on pain. "And we know how you felt about him. And those others—how did you feel about them?"

"I felt nothing, really. It wasn't about feelings. It should have been about physical gratification."

"Did you feel a fire inside you that could only be extinguished by physical union with any of them?"

"Uh, no, nothing like that. But I didn't hate the sight of them. They didn't fire me up, but they didn't repulse me, either."

"So you were trying to force yourself to eat when you weren't hungry, things which from the scent and look of them, weren't appetizing at all. Is it any wonder you didn't enjoy your meal?"

She stared at him before hooting with laughter. "That's priceless. And perfect. I was trying to eat limp, taste-free, homogenous-looking veggies because I was told they were good for me."

"Limp, eh?" He watched her wipe tears away, stopped himself from gathering her up again. She needed to sort this out in her mind before he took it to the realm of the flesh, where even he had no experience. Not with what would happen between them. "And how did I make you feel when you first saw me? How am I making you feel now?"

Her eyes widened, wonder seeping in, inching away agitation. "I saw you, and everything around me…vanished. Everything inside me started…tingling. I ached every time you moved and spoke. It got so bad, I wanted to scream. But it was also so good. Incredible. Like everything was enhanced, like there was this super charge of…*life* powering me. You made me feel with parts of me I was unaware of. And it hasn't stopped since, not even when you weren't there. I have only to think of you for you to affect me. Even when something else forces itself into my focus, you exist here now…"

Her hands flew to her head, pressed convulsively, before cascading over her face, her neck, her breasts, her abdomen and then lower, where they crossed and stroked their way from her hips upward until she was hugging her own arms.

He felt as if she had taken him inside every part of her, had him wrapped around her now.

"You're everywhere, a burn my blood carries to every inch of skin, a pressure building inside me. And then you look at me, talk to me, and it all becomes overwhelming. Flames burst out wherever your gaze lands. Currents bolt through me at the sound of your voice, at your touch. But it's your desire that…that…" She stopped, consternation clenching her face. "I'm doing a lousy job here. I can't describe it. And that was the easy part, the physical one."

He did have superhuman powers. He bit back at the urges sinking their fangs in him, didn't devour her in one go per his original impulse. Even though he was almost certain he'd give her as explosive a pleasure as he'd get.

The "almost" part stopped him. That and the need to show her the truth. About herself. About what he felt for her. There'd be endless time later for all levels of unrestrained mating.

He moved until his thigh brushed hers. Her chest heaved, her nipples conquering the thickness of her blouse through her open jacket. The creaminess of her skin had long disappeared in a tide of pink. Her lips were glazed with the flush of blood, skin taut over swelling flesh. His mental possession was doing this to her. He had the power to make her feel he was ravaging her for real just by imagining it so fiercely.

His forefinger skimmed her nose, her lips, down, until it rested at the edge of a now-visible cleavage, tormented them both with gossamer glimpses of what would be. "So when you feel all that, what do you expect it would be like with me?"

She moaned. "I-I don't know, okay? I just need to feel you, be with you."

He held her at arm's length. He couldn't just grab her. He had to prove to her that she was a sensual being of the highest order, attuned to such a level of sensitivity only a specific vibe—his—would release her potential, that any other's had been bound to grate, to even injure.

Yet he couldn't just claim that she'd been made for him, as he was now certain. He could only show her. And how he would.

But she was looking at him as if he'd stuck a knife in her gut. She wrenched herself from his detaining hands, almost ran away. He was so surprised that she was in his reception area, scooping up her briefcase when he caught up with her.

He put himself between her and the elevator. He had to be careful here. He didn't know what was upsetting her now.

"Any hope you'll explain where you think you're going?"

"Away. Before I mutilate the mood I just murdered."

That was the one thing he hadn't extrapolated as a reason for her sudden flight. Her surprises would never cease.

"I bet when you spent all this time cajoling me, you thought you were in for hot sex, not a sex therapy session with a thirty-year-old frigid divorcée." She took a step back, preparing to circumvent him. "No harm done, though. I hope. So—"

He dragged her to him, slammed her length against his, the collision a need, a must. Her briefcase slapped the floor as she arched into him, a carnal sound keening from her, her hands clawing an anchor in his flesh.

He wanted her to sink in all the way, penetrate him to the bone. His growl sounded feral as he snatched her off her feet, aching at how totally she distrusted her influence, how she'd been sought out only by men who had dealt her self-esteem and expectations of others one blow after another. It only made her trust in him that much more precious.

He captured her hands, withdrew enough to take one to his

heart, the other to the erection that hadn't subsided since he'd seen her. "So…which part of me seems not in the mood, *bellissima?*"

"This-this isn't just a typical male reaction? All my pathetic confessions didn't turn you off, here?" She freed the hand on his erection, pressed it to his head.

He pressed back, showing her he needed her assuagement. "I don't have male reactions if 'here' doesn't sanction them. And none of what you told me was pathetic. It ranged from criminal to inept on the men's side, and tragic to futile on yours. But I am honored beyond expression that when it came to me, you knew, like I did, that nothing that happened before applies to us. And it doesn't. This *is* us, and you have nothing to worry about. Not now, not ever." He turned his lips into her palm, planted his pledge. "You'll find only pampering and pleasure in my bed, support and protection everywhere else. I promise."

She surged forward, tears brimming over, and hugged breath out of him. "Oh, Durante, just take me. Take me before I wake up."

He threw his head back in exultation and relief. "This is one dream we're not waking up from. This I promise, too."

And she did something that made his whole being quiver as if it were about to explode.

She curled up against his heart and subsided. The extent of trust in the gesture almost brought him to his knees with emotions he'd never experienced. Gratitude, humility.

He crushed her to him, drank her down to her last moan. She only gave more, rubbed against him, opened her lips over any part she could reach of him and her legs as far as her pencil-slim skirt would allow, offering all the exquisiteness and passion that was her. He wanted to probe her, go berserk on finding her soaking, burning, crazy for everything he'd do to her. Then he wanted to do it all.

But something niggled at him. Something vital. He couldn't remember what. His mind had shut down, her arousal hitting him like a full-body blow. He'd better put the plan he'd just come up with into action, keep her with him until he remembered. He held her off, cupped her face. "Tell me, *Gabriella mia,* how do you feel about flying?"

Gabrielle had said she felt fine. About flying. And Durante had kissed more of her sanity away before walking out.

He now returned, a force of nature enveloping her as he led her out to his soccer field of a veranda.

She squinted into the sun as it glowed red on its descent into the ocean. Flying, huh? Literally or figuratively?

She wouldn't put anything past him.

Then they turned a corner against the high-rise wind, and it all made sense. As much sense as finding herself staring back at the gleaming black vicious beauty crouching in the middle of a large yellow circle on the ground.

He had his own freaking copter and helipad right outside his veranda door! With seventy-foot rotors, a passenger compartment big enough for half a dozen people and an outer body right out of some sci-fi flick.

Which really figured. When you had a fleet of jets, why not a multimillion-dollar toy to avoid the hassle of traffic jams?

Durante strapped her with utmost care on board the futuristic vehicle, taking the pilot seat, performing all safety measures then launching them in the air. She felt she'd left her stomach on the ground, along with a few nerves that snapped as she had her first personal encounter with seeing land recede almost beneath her feet.

He touched her gently, as if he knew, as he always seemed to know what she felt. Then he seemed to remember something major.

He'd cleared the city and veered out over the endlessness of the ocean, when he looked at her with that tenderness she'd never seen in another man's eyes and murmured, so quietly that she was stunned to hear him over the drone of the rotors, "Are you safe?"

She nodded before she realized what he was talking about. *Then* she contemplated jumping out. She couldn't have this conversation. Yeah, right. And this reluctance had to be some new standard for stupidity.

She was willing to have sex with him, but not to discuss protection from its risks?

She forced herself to spill all she had to say on the subject in one go. "I am. In every way. Checked and rechecked, although I *never* neglected protection. I also protected myself just in case. Measures still in place. I'm also at a safe time. I'm certain."

He made her breathing difficulties worse when he murmured, "I'm safe, too. I never neglect protection. But I can't even think of using it with you. I want to feel you without barriers and scorch you with my pleasure as you scorch me with yours." When she gurgled something he turned to her, serious, placating. "Don't feel under any pressure to agree. I'm just telling you how I feel. I'll arrange for protection to be delivered—"

"I don't want you to use it, either," she blurted out.

His eyes flared his satisfaction. It was all she could do to draw in enough air to keep from passing out.

In less than fifteen minutes she saw their destination. His yacht, moored miles offshore.

He landed on the uppermost deck where they'd had their first conversation on board. He turned off the motor, jumped out and was at her side in what felt like a flash, undid her belt and carried her down. She let him. She couldn't have walked if she tried.

He put his lips to her forehead as the sun dipped into the water, setting in a conflagration of color.

Suddenly the languorous spell of the moment fractured. He was putting her down, tenderly, languidly, but still letting her go. He took a few steps backward, the crimson rays of the departing sun striking turquoise lasers off his eyes.

Then he slowly, oh so slowly undid his tie.

She watched every movement of his large, beautiful hands, his corded neck as he flexed it and pulled the tie from around it, then his sculpted fingers as they finally held the tie away from his body, like a magician showing his audience the setup of his trick before he executed it. He let the tie go.

It plummeted, the silk sighing as it hit the deck.

He licked his lips, made her feel as if he'd licked hers then continued down the trail his eyes traveled down her middle. "Your turn."

Ten

Gabrielle shot a panicked look around, the warmth of the June day seeming to rise into raging heat instead of cooling with the sunset.

"Here?" she gulped.

"We have the place and the ocean to ourselves, *bellissima*."

So this was what he'd arranged during those minutes away.

It thrilled her that he gave her this freedom from scrutiny. It also terrified her, how much she wanted to take advantage of it, lose every inhibition. She wanted to attack him with kisses, but…

What if it *was* her? What if even wanting him this…terribly, she still felt nothing? Where would she be then?

Where she'd be anyway, eventually. Out of his life. So she just had to take what she could. Whatever the outcome.

As for what to take off, the logical thing was her jacket.

She was done doing things logically. Her logic had messed up her life so far. It was obviously essentially flawed. And logic said this couldn't be happening. But it was. And how. So to hell with it.

Elation simmered from her bones outward as she slowly, oh so slowly took off…her watch.

His face blazed in wicked delight when she let it fall to the deck, simulating his actions to the last move.

"Tormentress," he rumbled, took off his cufflinks.

She raised him her earrings. He surrendered his phone. She reciprocated with her hair clip. He threw down his checkbook.

The challenge arced between them in currents of elation and stimulation. She'd never laughed so freely with anyone. Or at all. And to be laughing even as longing melted her insides— *that* was unreal. And yet it felt like the only real thing she'd ever experienced.

Then she was out of nongarment things. He wasn't. The man *was* a magician. He had to be pulling all that stuff out of thin air. Her shoes went, then her jacket. When it was her blouse's turn, he moved closer. He took one step forward and something new off for each button she undid. Then all the buttons were undone and he was a breath away. The blouse hung open, still revealing nothing. She quivered. "Your turn."

"It's still your turn. With the last button, it comes off."

Her hands trembled uncontrollably as she pushed her blouse off. Then she was in her skirt and bra, unable to look at him, afraid to document his reaction, cringing inside.

What if he thought her breasts too big? Ed had said they were grotesque, unbalanced for her body. What if he preferred slimmer women? Different proportions? What if…?

A shockwave swept through her. Her eyes flew to his face.

She might have been alarmed at the eruption of testosterone blasting off him, the carnal ferocity in his features, if it hadn't gratified her, aroused her to the point of near-frenzy.

He tore off his jacket, muscles rippling, his whole body expanding. Then he hissed, "Next."

She expended the remnants of her coordination undoing her skirt.

Durante's nostrils flared, his gaze pouring heat over her, his chest rising and falling as if with exertion. He flicked open the first button of his shirt, hissed again, "Next."

She fumbled her bra open, instinctively held it in place.

"Let it drop, *bellissima*."

She did, whimpered. With the relief of releasing her swollen breasts from the imprisonment of the bra that had grown stifling. His jaw muscles worked as he undid another button then dropped to his knees, hands spanning her hips in a girdle of fire, his fingers hooking into her panties. "And last."

By the time the torturous sweep of lace and steel fingers skimmed her toes, she was panting. His hands reversed their path, inflaming her flesh with raw need. Then they stilled, an inch from her core.

He raised eyes like incendiary precious stones. *"Divina, preciosa mia…divina."*

He bent his awesome head to her flesh, suckled and nibbled her thighs and abdomen, moving higher like a starving man who didn't know where to start his feast. Her fingers convulsed in the wealth of his silky hair, pressed his face to her flesh in an ecstasy of torment, unable to take the stimulation, unable to get enough.

He took her breasts in hands that trembled, pressed them, weighed them, kneaded and nuzzled them as if they were the most amazing things he'd ever felt. Tears broke through her fugue of arousal. "You said fast and ferocious…*please*…"

"There's been a change in plan. The first two times will be torturously slow. We'll get to fast and ferocious the third time. Or maybe the fourth. Definitely the fifth."

She watched his head move against her breasts, heard her pleas thicken as his tongue and teeth turned the flesh she'd always thought sensitive to discomfort or pain into an instrument of unbearable pleasure. He tasted and nipped and murmured wonder and hunger, circled the center of her distress. If it wasn't for the ocean air cooling as the sun disappeared, she might have spontaneously combusted. Then his hands moved away and his tongue and teeth strayed over her…

This was nothing like she'd expected or imagined. Every squeeze had the exact force, each rub and nip and dig the exact roughness to extract maximum pleasure from her every nerve ending. He layered sensations with each press and bite, until she felt devoured, until she was overloading. Something was burning inside her. She undulated against him feverishly, pressing her clamoring flesh against any part of him in mindless pursuit of assuagement. Only then did he drag a rough, electrocuting hand between her thighs, teasing and tormenting his way to her core. The heel of his thumb found her outer lips at the same moment the damp furnace of his mouth clamped over a throbbing nipple. Sensation slashed her nerves.

He supported her collapsing weight, carried her to rest against the railing where they'd stood that night, one knee beneath her buttock, one between her thighs.

"I wanted to do this to you that first night…" He slid two fingers between her molten inner lips, stilled at her entrance. "I wanted to see you like this, on fire, open, hunger shaking you apart. Then I wanted to do this…"

He again dropped to his knees, spread her legs, placed one after the other over his shoulders, opening her to his eyes and touch. He inhaled her, rumbled like a lion maddened at the scent of his female in heat, then blew a gust of acute sensation over her quivering flesh. Her hips bucked, her last "please" morphing into a squeal. It became a shriek when he pumped two fingers into her, in a slow, slow glide. The sunset turned into darkest night as she convulsed, pleasure slamming through her in desperate surges.

Her sight burst back to an image from a fantasy. Him,

clothed, kneeling between her legs, her, naked, splayed open over his shoulders, in the midst of an ocean that did feel as if it were their own.

Then, among the mass of aftershocks she'd become, she felt it. His fingers still filling her, pumping her, beckoning inside her.

Her gasping mouth widened as his tongue joined in, licked from where his fingers were buried inside her upward, circling her bud until she heard her voice sobbing pleas again. His lips locked on her core. She bucked, pressed her burning flesh to his mouth, opening herself fully to his double sensual assault, bewilderment shooting through her as each glide and graze and pull and thrust sent hotter lances skewering through her, as if she hadn't just had the most intense orgasm of her life. And before she could draw a full breath, she was in the throes again, quaking and screaming with an even more violent release.

She tumbled from the explosive peak, drained, sated. Stupefied. What had just happened?

Her drugged eyes sought his, as if for answers. Even in the twilight they glowed azure, heavy with hunger and satisfaction.

"You are the most magnificent thing I have ever touched or tasted. I will never get enough of you."

Suddenly she was hungrier, the emptiness where she needed him gnawing at her. She writhed, her hands running over his lush hair. "Can we skip to fast and ferocious now…*please?*"

He chuckled against her inner thighs, cupping her, desensitizing her. "But those two times don't count. The ones I promised will be with me inside you, riding you to ecstasy."

Her mouth dropped open.

Before she could respond, he swept her up in his arms, headed inside the yacht, taking a route she hadn't seen before.

In minutes he entered a huge, elaborately furnished suite with marble floors, Persian carpets and soaring ceilings that traversed two decks. Must be the master suite he'd mentioned. A gigantic, circular bed draped in royal blue satin crouched beneath a domed skylight that glowed with the last tendrils of twilight. Oil lamps blazed everywhere, swathing everything in golden mystery and intimacy.

Sinking deeper in the sensory overload realm, she tried to drag him on top of her as he put her on the bed. He sowed kisses over her clinging arms, withdrew, stood back looking down at her.

"Meravigliosa," he breathed. "Do you realize how amazing you are?" Elation, embarrassment and disbelief gurgled in the back of her throat. "Do you want to *see* how amazing I think you are?"

That got her voice working. "Yes, please."

And he started to strip. And if their stripping game had had her begging, his as he exposed each sculpted inch almost had her passing out with the pressure of anticipation. She'd been right the night of the ball. He did have the body of a higher being.

He was down to his boxers when he turned into the light… and she saw it. The scar. A two-inch, puckered line across the smooth perfection of his skin. Negligible, really.

A wave of nausea hit her. She scrambled up on hands and knees, hugged him convulsively around the waist, pressed her trembling lips to where he'd been hurt. A few inches to the right, where its perpetrator had aimed, and the knife could have caused untold damage. Could have snuffed out all this uniqueness and vitality.

He smoothed his hands over her hair. "Don't think what-ifs, *amore*. I'm fine and that's what matters, *sì?*"

He understood, as he always seemed to. She hugged him harder, opened her mouth over his wound, as if she could drain away the pain of the memory. He groaned, pressed her against his flesh, surrendering to her need to heal him. She couldn't *bear* it if something happened to him. She moaned the dread out loud.

"Nothing will happen to me." His eyes were serious, pledging. Then they suddenly melted in sensuality and teasing as he rubbed her breasts with the silk-roughened steel of his thighs. "Except maybe a heart attack from this display of beauty."

She gazed up at him, her insides trembling. How she *wanted* him. In every way.

He stepped back and dropped his boxers, released the proof of how much *he* wanted *her.* In that way, at least.

She'd felt that he was big. But this…she'd never seen anything half as huge. Or anywhere near as beautiful.

Her senses swam. The spike of desire combined with shock of intimidation almost dragged her under.

One thing brought her back to full focus. The need to feel his manhood, touch it, smell it, taste it. She'd never wanted to do that, had even been repulsed when she'd imagined doing it, to other men. She shook with wanting to do it to him.

He let her hold him, shuddered at her touch, groaned at the flick of her tongue, growled when she overcame the last shred of inhibition and opened her mouth wide over the satin crown. She moaned around his hot hardness, lost in the pleasure of him. Then she leaned back to look up at him.

"Oh, Durante," she whispered. "You're the most magnificent thing I've ever touched or tasted, too."

His fingers dug into her scalp, shooting pleasure to every hair root. "Take your every pleasure from me, always. But I need to pleasure you now, with my body."

She relinquished him as if all her strings had been cut, melted onto her back awash with the enormity of craving and anxiety.

She'd know now. Her body was weeping in an agony of need for him. If she didn't feel pleasure with him, it was hopeless.

But he'd already given her pleasure like she'd never known. She truly didn't care if she couldn't feel anymore. She just needed to feel him inside her before she disintegrated.

He prowled over her, kissed his way from her toes to her center to her breasts to her lips until his bulk pressed between her trembling thighs. He cupped her buttocks, touched the head of his erection to her entrance, nudged her, bathing himself in her wetness. Her hands pressed his biceps convulsively, her intimate flesh fluttering around him, begging him to enter. His eyes roiled with a dizzying mixture of lust and tenderness as he finally pumped his hips, breached her tightness with persistent yet restrained pressure. Then he was there, where she needed him, penetrating her in a long, languorous thrust.

The expansion of her tissues around his erection went on and on. The fullness sharpened into an ache that became almost a pain. Darkness danced at the periphery of her vision.

She gasped, thrashed. He stilled, started to withdraw. She felt she'd implode if he left her body, grabbed him, arms and legs and core. "No...don't...stay inside me...please."

"You took half of me and started shaking. Let me move *bellissima,* we'll take it easier."

Half of him? She slackened her muscles inside and out, and he pushed up on extended arms. She looked down, open-mouthed. He *was* only halfway inside her. Would she be able to take all of him? But she needed to. She wanted him to shatter her with his full invasion.

She fell back, shuddering, panting. "No, do it, please. I need you inside me all the way, hard, *please...*"

With a pained groan, he bent, suckled her nipples, sending a million arrows of pleasure to her core with every pull, squeezing more fiery arousal from her depths. He had her mindlessly pumping her hips up at him, begging for impalement with fevered sobs before he succumbed, slid back into her.

This time he didn't stop, kept invading her, stretching her, the head of his shaft pressing against her internal flesh, setting off a string of charges that buried her under layers of sensations she'd never felt before, a buildup that seemed to originate from her every cell and radiate from his flesh all at once, a pressure that distilled desperation into a physical symptom. He stopped his onslaught only when he reached her cervix, and everything in her seemed to compact into a pinpoint of gravity for an unendurable moment before detonating outward. She shattered.

Her hips heaved, so hard that she almost lifted him in the air, the sensations exploding from her depths so fierce that she couldn't scream, couldn't breathe, not for the first dozen clenches of release as the excruciating pleasure ripped through her.

Then she screamed and screamed as it went on and on. He withdrew then plunged, then again and again, riding her ecstasy, not letting it subside, building the pressure inside her again as he took her lips, thrust inside her mouth with his tongue, simulating the powerful thrusts of his manhood until another tsunami built, hovered, then crashed over her.

This time she screamed with the first crashing chord of the climax, her muscles squeezing the hardness and girth pistoning satisfaction into her, convulsing around it, drenching it with wave after wave of pleasure.

He rose above her, muscles taught, eyes tempestuous, face seizing with the pleasure of possessing her, pleasuring her, his beauty supernatural in the extreme. Then he threw his head back and roared as every muscle in his body locked, his erection pressing to her womb, gushing his own release to mingle with hers, long, hard jets that ignited her nerves into one more conflagration.

The last thing she knew was that aftershocks could hit a level of excitement all their own, that they were more draining than the peaks of pleasure…

Gabrielle stirred in cottony bliss, opened her eyes.

The gibbous moon came into focus. It hung in the piece of sky framed in the skylight above. She was being stroked like a cat from face to thigh. She was purring.

Durante purred, too, the deep rumbles of the sated, triumphant lion that he was. He had a right to be. She'd thought he'd given her the orgasms of her life, that she'd never recharge enough to want sex ever again. But he'd aroused her to weeping again, before showing her that, a) she had buttons that only he knew how to push to give her shattering orgasms in succession, b) she recharged in record time and c) so did he.

"You were saying? This thing about being frigid?" he rumbled against her neck, his smile tickling her.

"Uh…it was clearly a case of misdiagnosis." She sounded like what she was. A woman who'd been savagely pleasured, had screamed herself hoarse in appreciation.

"One of vast proportions. You're the most sensuous, responsive creature imaginable, and your capacity for pleasure is limitless. But then, capacity is just a potential. It means nothing without the right touch to release it. Your body is a complex, extremely selective instrument of sensual delights. It responds only when everything satisfies you. As I do."

As only you will ever do, she almost blurted out. She bit it back.

It felt as if he were the first and only man she'd ever been with. Really been with. No man had ever taken her like that. She'd never accepted a man inside her like that. Beside his phenomenal size, stamina and rebound time, the things he'd done to her had been undreamed of. The way she'd responded, the way she'd opened herself to whatever he wished to do, had been something she hadn't imagined herself capable of.

But that was probably more info than he'd want to know. She'd better keep it light.

"You're in a league of your own, *bellissima.*"

"Look who's talking. You weren't kidding. Or bragging."

He chuckled, consumed her in a leisurely mating of mouths, smiling into the warmth and intimacy of the meld, soothing the soreness he'd inflicted, before moving down her body and performing the same healing ritual to the nipples she'd begged him to devour in the throes of ecstasy.

"Far from kidding or bragging, I actually downplayed things. I didn't want you to think you'd fallen into the clutches of a sex maniac and run off screaming."

"So you misled me about the nature of what awaited me, conned me onto my back, uh—among other positions—and made me scream there instead?"

"And how you scream. Every scream was like an intra-venous shot of aphrodisiac, shooting through my system to deluge my brain. I almost blew an artery."

"Good thing you have a safety valve."

"And it's going to come to my rescue constantly. Like now."

He pressed between the thighs that trembled apart for him, unable to bear those last moments as desire became pain before his hardness and heat filled her again, stretching her into mind-lessness, thrusting her to oblivion.

Pangs started to throb, dragging Gabrielle back from the void. She didn't want to float up from the realm of bliss, wanted to remain suspended there forever.

But the ache mounted, pushed against the lethargy, advanc-ing awareness through her body, until she realized.

Durante. She was wrapped up in him, virility made solid gold muscles, power and hunger and satisfaction made man. Her head was resting on his biceps; her lips were buried in his chiseled chest. Every inch of her was imprinted with his sleek, slightly hair-roughened silk-over-steel body.

The ache rose, changed texture to something she hadn't felt the many times she'd woken up to more lovemaking. This time it was different. This was the morning after the transfiguring night.

She had nothing to compare to what she'd shared with him. She hadn't even had morning-afters with her disappointments.

She couldn't leave this time. And it wasn't because she was in the middle of the ocean with no way to go home unless he took her. She wanted to stay, for as long as it was possible to stay, wanted to experience everything again, and more, with him.

He rumbled something deep and unbearably sexy as he threw one leg over both of hers, his arms sliding into the deep curve of her waist to her buttocks, hauling her against him, his erection, intact as ever. She was so ready again, or rather, still, it was embarrassing.

He took her mouth, took her breath and will away.

When he relinquished her lips to nibble his way down her face, her neck, she gasped, "*Buon giorno* to you, too."

His fingers probed her, slipped into her, circled her bud. She thrust her hips into his pleasuring, needing, desperate, just like that.

"It isn't a good morning, *Gabriella mia*. It's a *magnifico giorno*, the most magnificent morning in history." He turned her onto her back, looked at her as if he couldn't decide which part of her to ravish first. "And do you know what your magnificence did to me, besides the loud and obvious? I dreamed all night. And I remember each second of every dream." He quickened his fondling. "Now I'm going to reenact each and every one."

She gasped as he drove her over the edge. And she knew. Her anxiety had no root in reality. There could never be a letdown with Durante. Only soaring.

And if a voice rasped that a fall from such heights could be far more devastating, she stifled it as she gave all of herself up to the wonder of him, of what they'd found together.

Eleven

Gabrielle watched Giancarlo close the door behind him, a smile hovering on her lips.

For the past two weeks it had become a ritual. She'd arrive at Durante's penthouse, he'd open the door for her and disappear.

She'd torn through her work like she'd been doing every day, the work for which she'd found her passion and enthusiasm miraculously resurrected, to hurtle back to Durante.

The day after they'd returned from his yacht, she'd left the next morning, returned eight hours later. She hadn't stayed the night since. Durante hadn't asked her to. But they spent their afternoons and evenings together, making love and every other thing under the sun before he escorted her to her apartment.

She couldn't believe she'd thought herself frigid. Evidence said she was bordering on nymphomania. A condition with a specific activator by the name of Durante D'Agostino.

Now she had only to think of him for her body to gnaw at her with the need for him. He had only to touch her, sometimes just suckle or caress or blow his breath on any of her triggers, and those were many and increasing, to unleash her first release. But the shattering climaxes he gave her when he took her boggled her mind.

Not that it was all about or even mainly about sex between them. They reveled in each other in every other way. Every day brought ever-expanding harmony and deepening involvement in each other's lives. This evening was another milestone. He was introducing her to his friends. Or as he'd said, "producing them for her inspection and approval."

"Stay."

Durante's gruff whisper forked through her.

Not from surprise. She'd felt his approach. She'd probably felt it when it was still an intention forming in his mind. She'd waited for him to initiate the reconnection, set the pace and tone of this encounter as he had every other so far.

She had no idea what this one word could mean. She'd just come in.

Could he…? She didn't dare think what he meant. So she quipped, "Again with the canine references. But then you already got me to roll over and beg."

His eyes crinkled as he pulled her to him, tenderness mixing with rough sensuality and possession into a mind-melting concoction. "You got me to beg, too. I can even do back flips and walk on my hands, at your order."

He bent, opened his mouth over the pulse in her neck, suckled her in long pulls as if he were drinking her. Fireworks exploded inside her, followed by a gush of readiness and the need for him to fill her again.

But his friends were coming in minutes.

That was logic's voice. Her body's said *take all you can, while you can.*

She obeyed it, moaned, "Take me, Durante *bello,* take me…"

He raised his head, instant ferocity taking over his face,

thinning his lips. He snatched her skirt up to her waist, took her by the buttocks and spread her around his hips. He staggered with her to the nearest erect surface as she clung to him, disintegrating with the firebomb of hunger he'd detonated inside her. He set her against something that rattled as he freed himself, tore her panties out of the way, slid her up her support to scale his length. She felt the head of his erection at her moist entrance, keened. He let her crash down on him, just as he thrust up, piercing her. It took no more than feeling him forging through her to shatter her. She shrieked with the sledgehammer of orgasm, convulsing around his shaft as if she were imploding.

He growled into her mouth. "*Sì, Gabriella, sì*, take all of me, take your pleasure of me, come all over me."

The orgasm raged on and on until he roared and slammed her against the rattling support, his release so powerful that she writhed, trembled, sobbed with the sensations. She went nerveless and he tightened his hold around her, still hard and twitching inside her. Her flesh quivered around him with the aftershocks of the profound release.

He took her slack mouth in carnal possession, blowing air into her breathless lungs, growling all the while, rocking gently again and again inside her, satisfying her to her last tremor. "*Siete magici, mi' bellezza…magici…*"

Her head flopped on his shoulder as she tried to get her nerves to spark. She needed to hold him, to revel in his existence, his magic. "It's you…you who are, *bello mio…*"

The bell rang.

Durante jerked. "*Maledizione.* I should have told Giancarlo to entertain them somewhere else until…" He swore again. "I should have known I wouldn't be able to last until they left to make love to you. I yearned for you all day, *Gabriella mia.*"

She moaned. "And I for you."

He took her lips, strode with her wrapped around him to his bathroom. He put her down gently on the huge platform of marble flanking the sink. Then he reluctantly, and so slowly, withdrew from her depths. She moaned at the ache of separation.

She groaned again at the sight of herself in the mirror behind him, at his brutal beauty and caring as he kneeled in front of her, intimately taking care of the evidence of their lovemaking, so her skirt wouldn't be stained. Then he rose to his feet and towered over her, his muscles rippling under his shirt as he struggled to straighten and smooth his pants.

"Take your time getting ready." He took her face in his hands, urgency rippling in the passion in his grip, his eyes. "But answer me first. Will you stay, *bellissima?*"

"Tonight, you mean?"

"I mean every night."

Gabrielle gazed across the room at Durante. He was putting on some music, laughing with his younger cousin, Eduardo. Her heart quivered. She'd said yes.

But…he'd said stay. Not live. Was there a difference?

"So how long have you known Durante, Gabrielle?"

She turned to the mahogany-haired, green-eyed woman so aptly named Jade. A few years younger than her, she judged, Jade glowed with that special vitality healthy pregnant women had. She and Eduardo were both floating on air. Their love for each other was almost visible, tangible.

Jade was also curious in the most innocuous way Gabrielle had ever experienced.

"Not long. We met three weeks ago."

"Bet it feels like three years."

Now, how did she know that?

Jade answered her unvoiced question, "It was like that with me and Eduardo. Did you have a tempestuous beginning, too?"

Gabrielle laughed. "So there *is* a pattern with the D'Agostino princes."

As she laughed, she felt rather than saw Durante stiffen. Her eyes flew to his, locked, mingled, mated across the huge space until the room flooded with tension so carnal, so predatory and proprietary, she felt as if he were inside her again, occupying her, dominating her, dissolving her in satiation.

The volcanic exchange lasted only a couple of seconds before Eduardo drew his focus away again as Jade caught hers.

Jade sighed. "But they're worth every heartache. At least I know Eduardo is literally worth dying for. How's your Durante?"

Gabrielle spluttered with laughter. "You say that as if you're asking me 'How's your steak.'"

Jade grinned, her beauty blazing a few notches higher with the unbridled expression. "They are far more edible than the juiciest steak, aren't they? Not that I think Durante could be anywhere near Eduardo in tastiness. Eduardo is pure ambrosia."

Gabrielle laughed again. "Fair enough. To me Durante is on a celestial menu of his own."

"You love him."

The statement hit Gabrielle between the eyes.

She struggled not to lurch with its power, its certainty, murmured, "It's too early for anything like that."

"Uh-uh, it isn't. Not with these men."

And "these men" were heading toward them now. Eduardo was a gorgeous male, Gabrielle acknowledged, but in her eyes, Durante was far beyond that. He was above comparison.

"Durante seems…younger," Jade said as the men progressed slowly across the room, still talking but with their eyes on the women. "I haven't seen him laughing—hell, I haven't even seen him smile—since I first met him six months ago. And because of Eduardo's friendship and business with him, I've seen him a lot. I didn't know he *could* laugh. I thought he came without the laughter software." She turned to Gabrielle. "But you reformatted him."

Gabrielle chuckled again. Almost everything Jade said tickled her. "Ah, Jade, isn't reformatting reserved for the hard drive?"

"What's this about reformatting and hard drives?" Durante came to Gabrielle's side, sat on the couch's armrest, pulled her to him, kissed the top of her head, her temple, her jaw. Then he murmured in her ear so softly he almost didn't produce sound. "Look at me like that and I'll haul you to bed and hard drive your software and to hell with them."

She looked up at him. Yes, like *that*. She pulled him down, whispered in his mouth. "You didn't need a bed, or much time, for that in extremely fresh memory. I'm sure you can manage with them here and not in hell."

He bit down on one of her tormenting lips. "When we serve dessert, you'll skip it. You're having me."

Eduardo had mirrored Durante's actions with Jade, as if they'd agreed to. After he let her up from a clinging kiss he belatedly answered Durante's question. "That's *mia bella Giada,* always talking computers. Watch that you don't get her started on programming, though."

"You're the only one who makes me blurt out code, *amore*." She beamed at him, then turned to Durante. "We were talking about you."

Gabrielle held her breath. Jade was clearly even more outspoken than Durante had complained. Would she blurt out that she believed Gabrielle loved him?

She almost deflated to the floor when Jade related only the part about his missing laughter software and the subsequent comments.

Durante laughed, demonstrating his newly restored sense of humor. "That's one of many things Gabrielle reformatted about me."

Jade's grin grew devilish. "I saw her reformatting your arrogance, in public. On YouTube."

Eduardo grinned at his bride conspiratorially. "*Sì,* and from the marks on your cheek, I'd say that in a previous scene, she reformatted it, too."

Durante looked at Gabrielle. After a moment of stunned silence, they burst into howls of laughter.

Raucous ribbing was exchanged in the aftermath of their fit, and from then on, the evening flowed with the harmony of the men's deep friendship and the women's instant rapport.

All through, each man pampered his woman with every gesture and word and touch. Jade reciprocated her demonstrative husband's affection with gusto. Gabrielle, feeling the odd man out, the one who didn't share the same status as them, reciprocated Durante's doting but wasn't as spontaneous. Not as she longed to be.

For Jade had been right.

She might not have let herself say the words, even to herself, but she'd fallen flat on her face in love with him from that first night. She'd been stumbling deeper with each breath ever since. She didn't see an end to her plummet.

But she'd effectively been lying to him.

She didn't know how to come clean about how this had started without implicating his father per her promise.

It was so unfair. Why should she risk spoiling what they had now, when it had never been her fault, this inadvertent deception? It didn't matter how it had all started, as he'd said. It had ceased to be a mission on his father's behalf, or on her company's, the moment she'd laid eyes on him.

At the evening's end, something disturbing nagged at her.

The difference. Between "stay" and "live."

"Stay" might mean that he didn't feel the same about her as she did for him. That he'd sooner or later have enough of her. And there would be no point in confessing anything, anyway.

She tried not to hear the voices that said if he ended it, she'd be far worse off than she'd been before she'd met him. That this time, there would be no hope of finding a point to anything ever again.

Twelve

Gabrielle was balancing on the edge of the springboard.

She flashed Durante a grin that turned the night into day, one all but yelling "Look, look."

As if he could do anything else. His gaze clung to her every move, as it always did, his heart in a state of constant expansion.

Once she was certain she had his full attention, she looked ahead, concentration settling over her face, showing him another side of her, the determined woman who could and did succeed in anything she endeavored. She tensed her body so that every muscle in her toned firmness was on alert, stood on her tiptoes, raised her arms. Then she dipped her weight, jumped once, twice, launching higher in the air with the elastic recoil of the board, then on the third launch, she catapulted into a backward somersault, tucking her whole body in a ball, revolving in two full turns before unfolding fully, her whole body stretched and straight like a human missile, entered the water fingertips first, cutting the surface like a laser beam. She didn't splash a drop.

He sprang to his feet the second she was submerged, ran to the edge of the pool, clapping and hooting, elation tumbling in his blood. She broke the surface with a smile as huge as his, swept around and around in the water like a giddy mermaid, reveling in his adulation, taking her bows.

Unable to wait, he plunged after her, surfaced with her wrapped around him. He squeezed her, ravaged her with clinging, smiling kisses, which she reciprocated with ardor enough to make him steam the pool. He slid his lips up to her ear. "So you're an Olympic diver and you never told me."

She giggled. "Nothing so exalted. I used to be my school's diving champion, got so far as the regional competitions. Won me some gold medals in those. But the last time I saw a spring-board was seven years ago. I wanted to show you one of the few things that made me feel alive. I practiced while you took care of your business so I wouldn't disgrace myself. And it's true. It is like riding a bike. My body will curse me tomorrow, but it was worth it." She yelped with the excess adrenaline still coursing in her blood. "It felt *great!* I thought I'd grown old and creaky."

"You will never be that. And you will never again neglect your passions and your talents, *Gabriella mia.* Promise me."

She nodded, her eyes blasting him with unadulterated appreciation, for his solicitude, for everything that he was. She made him feel treasured to his last cell. Just as he treasured her.

He swept her into his arms, swam on his back in leisurely strokes with her nestled at his side, the largest part of his soul. His gaze swept through the now-open plexi roof at another moonless, star-blazing night. Exotic plants teemed at the pool's periphery forming an oasis in the middle of the ocean. Their oasis. He'd changed his mind about donating this boat. He was going to re-outfit it for them. He reveled in being with her in the freedom of such a setting, such a huge personal space.

He luxuriated in feeling her this way, through the silk medium of perfect-temperature water, her satin resilience and strength tapping into and feeding his own in a closed circuit of harmony. This had long surpassed any heaven he'd ever heard about.

What they shared was something he'd never imagined there was to be shared. He'd witnessed family and friends finding their soulmates, but he'd never believed he'd find his own. Now, he hadn't just found his in her, he'd also been given a second chance when he'd wasted the first that fate had handed him. He still woke up in cold sweat thinking he'd forever alienated her only to subside, nerve-wracked and kissing-the-floor thankful at finding her curled up next to him.

Only one thing disturbed him. Every now and then he felt some reticence from her. He could think of only one reason for that unease. The speed with which everything had happened.

He didn't feel that they'd gone too fast. He felt everything had unfolded in total leisure. Time stretched, widened, deepened when they were together. The month since they'd met felt like a year. More. He couldn't remember a time when he didn't know her. Didn't want to remember. For what was there to remember before her?

But he forced himself to let her set the pace. It might look like he'd rushed her to move in with him in ten days. But in his view, he'd *waited* ten days. He'd wanted her to stay from that first night. He didn't have the least doubt. He knew. She was the one he'd thought he'd never find. The one he'd been made for.

He kissed her again. "Thank you for sharing your dive with me, *bellissima*. Share everything with me, always."

She enveloped him in the contentment, the serenity and certainty only her embrace had ever imbued him with. Then she suddenly wriggled, broke his hold, kicked away.

She giggled as he gave pursuit. She was such a strong swimmer he almost didn't need to slow down for her to beat him to the other end of the pool. She pulled herself out in one agile move, stood there in her flame-colored, one-piece torture device of a swimsuit, grinning down at him, before she ran to the dinner table he'd had set for them before he'd sent everyone off the yacht. He never wanted anyone around when he was with her.

Tonight of all nights, it had to be just them.

He followed, taking his time to get his fill of watching her as she dried herself in brisk movements that grew languid, sensuous as he neared. He kept walking until he imprinted her from breast to calf, gathered her to him, cherished her with caresses and kisses as she stroked him dry.

"About sharing…" she purred against his neck, rubbing against him, stoking the fire perpetually raging for her. "I keep realizing I told you my life's sob stories in embarrassing detail. Whereas you told me outlines. Very unbalanced, if you ask me. I feel fully naked, with you with only your tie undone."

"But you love it that way."

"That is a supreme truth only equaled by the fact that I am just as addicted to watching your mind-blowing stripteases."

He raised an eyebrow, pseudo-suspicious. "You want to get everything out of me so you can help me sort through my issues, don't you?"

Her eyes melted with tenderness. "Got me. Is it so bad to want to do for you a fraction of what you did for me?"

He stared at her. Would she ever cease to surprise him? To do and say exactly the right thing, at the right moment?

He sat down in one of the chaise longues where they sun-bathed in seclusion, brought her down straddling him, wrapped her in his arms, rested his forehead on her bosom.

Sì, it was the right moment to share all of him with her.

Durante nuzzled her like a lion would his mate before resting his ear on her heart. The poignancy of the revealing gesture swamped her, the so freely demonstrated admission that he needed the solace of her.

He stroked her back rhythmically, making her insides quiver with bliss. Then he started talking.

"Everything was perfect, or so I thought, until I was eleven. Looking back, things were never anywhere near perfect between my parents. Or with my mother. She had this…irrepressible energy. It was sometimes painful to watch her, like…looking at the sun. But she always dimmed around my father. I didn't give it much thought until she dimmed all the time, during her pregnancy with my sister. After Clarissa was born it was like she forgot she had other children. I was hurt by her neglect, more on my brother Paolo's behalf. She explained that I was a big boy, could take care of my brother, and I needed to be with my father more, while her baby girl needed her. I conceded that, thought it the natural order of things. And for years I got involved in my own life. But by age eighteen I could no longer overlook it. My mother had become unbalanced, one day manic, the next in a stupor. I thought my father was not doing enough—or anything—to stop her decline.

"Then I walked into her apartments unannounced one day and saw her…hitting Clarissa. Really hitting her. Clarissa had curled up in a ball on the ground as my mother beat her. But what really horrified me was that Clarissa's cowering felt habitual. This wasn't the first time. I charged in, overpowered my mother, and she kicked and writhed in my hold like a madwoman. I could no longer find my mother in her eyes. She spat in my face, told me I was so like my father she couldn't bear to look at me. I was… devastated. I…hated her at that moment."

A gasp tore through her. He pressed her closer, lost in the past. "But what I felt didn't matter. Only Clarissa did. I faced my father. I didn't care what was going on between him and my mother, but I wouldn't see Clarissa hurt. He swore he'd been ignorant of this, that he'd never let my mother lay a hand on Clarissa again. I left Castaldini the day Father took Clarissa to his apartments. I returned periodically to check that she remained safe from our mother's mood swings.

"She was. For those moods stopped swinging, became a

steady downward descent. Until the day she died. I came home for her funeral, almost didn't recognize the woman in the coffin.

"After the funeral I had a long conversation with my father. He said he'd tried his utmost to help her over the years, but she'd been unapproachable about undergoing therapy, had accused him of trying to make her admit that she was crazy.

"I went to her apartments looking for jewelry and personal items that I thought Clarissa should have and would never think of taking for herself. After the abusive period passed, Clarissa had become closer to our mother, sort of her keeper, and I wanted her to have some reminders of better times before mental illness took our mother away from us, to equalize the anguish and sadness that had taken over Clarissa's memories of her. And I found my mother's diary.

"The entries started with her discovery of her pregnancy with Clarissa. Some were written in…blood." Gabrielle gasped, squeezed him as hard as her heart contracted. "Page after page, year after year of agony, of obsession, of unbearable feelings of betrayal. I could almost hear her laments blast me from the pages. How she'd given him her life, her soul, her heart, given birth to the flesh of his flesh, and he'd told her she'd always been a convenience, a means to an end, that his true love was a woman who might not be a queen but was the queen of his heart, a woman she wasn't fit to be a servant to. The last entry made it clear that my mother intended to end her life."

Gabrielle panted, her heart threatening to punch a hole in her chest.

"I stormed to my father, hurled the diary at him. It *had* been him all the time. He *had* systematically destroyed my mother while he earned our sympathy for suffering such a wife. I demanded to know who the woman was whose comparison he'd used to dismantle my mother's soul. He said it had been her delusions talking. But I saw the lie in his eyes. And I told him he'd taken my mother from me, from all of us, pushed her until she'd killed herself, that I'd leave Castaldini and I'd return only when he was dead."

She crushed him to her as if she'd take him into her, hide him from hurt, and sobbed. Until she felt she'd come apart.

"Shh, don't cry, *preziosa mia,* it's all right."

She hiccupped a syncopation of incredulity before bursting into even more hacking sobs. *He* was soothing *her?*

He was, kept gentling her, murmuring to her as if she were a frightened child, until his caring and consideration became too much to bear.

She pushed away, wiping angrily at the tears blinding her, winced when her vision cleared. She'd soaked his hair and face.

She blotted them frantically. He caught and kissed her hands. She surged to him, raining kisses all over his face, quavered, "You've got this wrong. *I'm* supposed to comfort *you.*"

"And you did, *amore mio.* With every beat of your heart as I recounted the story, as it pounded, tripped, held its breath then burst with empathy and compassion."

"But what good is that when you have all this pain inside you? This way you've lost both your parents in ways worse than death…"

She stopped, couldn't breathe. King Benedetto *couldn't* be guilty of such cold-blooded abuse at all, let alone to the woman who had loved him to the point of self-destruction, his queen and mother of his children, could he? If he had, then he wasn't the man she'd believed him to be, didn't deserve to get Durante back. Worse, if that was how he treated those who loved him, what if he did the same to Durante? And he'd wanted *her* to convince him…

Sobs wracked her. "I can't *bear* it."

He took her face in his hands, stroked both thumbs over her cheeks, wiped away her tears and anguish. Then he began to sing.

"Vorrei che i tuoi occhi siano la mia prima luce al risveglio…"

I want your eyes to be the first light I see when I wake up every morning.

Everything stilled. The air filled with the magic that emanated from his lips, potent, unstoppable, the sound of power and virility and wonder. Of love.

Quakes started again, different in origin but just as devastating, as consuming. He continued his spell, deepening its destruction, spreading its restoration.

"E il profumo della tua pelle accompagni ogni mio passo... per sempre."

And the perfume of your skin to accompany my every step... forever.

"Vuoi percorrere il sentiero della vita insieme a me, amore?"

Will you walk your life's path with me, my love?

Then he fell silent. And she wept. Her first tears of wonder, of being moved by beauty to an extreme surpassing any pain.

Suddenly trepidation pushed aside the tenderness in his eyes.

She couldn't let him think her reaction wasn't one of extreme joy and enjoyment. She blurted out, "That's the most unbelievably, almost painfully beautiful thing I've ever heard. How did something like that not become an immortal hit?"

"Maybe because its writer wanted only one woman to hear it."

"You...?" Shock hurtled through her. *"Dio...Durante..."*

"Sposami, anima mia."

Marry me, my soul.

"Gabriella mia, mi vuoi sposare?"

Durante asked again. *Will you marry me?*

And nothing. Gabrielle was staring at him as if she'd suddenly stopped understanding Italian.

His certainty wavered. This didn't look like surprise. Not the pleasant kind. But...why? What could be so...shocking? Surely she'd known where all this was leading? But if she was...unpleasantly surprised, did that mean she didn't...?

No. He wouldn't speculate. Never again. No doubts. He'd ask, and she'd tell him the truth. She always told the truth.

"Gabrielle? Don't you have anything to say, *bellissima?*"

"Say? I-I can't think of anything…can't think…"

"Then tell me the first thing that jumped into your mind."

Her eyes were enormous, shock still expanding. "I-I thought I heard wrong, then I thought, it's only been a month. Three weeks, if you take away your famous Ten Days of Tantrum."

He stared at her for a moment. Then he hooted with laughter. "Ah, *preziosa mia,* I never laughed for real before you."

Her eyebrows shot up, her shock receding, her effort to match his teasing evident. "You want to marry me and make me your jester?"

"I want to marry you and make you my *everything.* My lover, my confidante, my friend, my ally, my psychoanalyst, my conscience, my perspective. As for how long we've known each other, you've known many people for years. Did that make you need them? Even like or tolerate them? Time isn't a factor here and you know it."

She nodded, shook her head, looking lost. "So time doesn't promote involvement, but lack of it makes said involvement's validity iffy. If…if in a few months' time, a year's, you still feel the same…"

"I will feel the same in sixty years' time. This is only going to deepen, as it has every second of the past month."

"You don't know that."

"You mean because no one knows what will happen in the future? But anything the future brings is irrelevant, because I am positive of one thing. Myself. In my thirty-eight years I have never even fancied myself in lust with any woman. I was waiting for you. From the first moment, it was like finding the missing parts of *m'anima e corpo*—my soul and body. You think I can go back to living without what makes me whole?" Pain streaked across her face. His heart compressed, the world going lightless. He groaned the unbearable fear. "Don't you feel the same, Gabrielle? Are the doubts yours?"

His heart almost ruptured in the moments before she gulped the breath she needed to cry out what made him breathe again. "No! God, no! I love you so much I have panic attacks with it sometimes. I-I just can't imagine having this, you, for always. I never thought happiness like this could be anything but temporary. I was waiting for you to…to have enough of me and…and…"

"Can I have enough of bliss? Of sustenance? Of air?"

"Durante…this is too much…too much…"

"Nothing is too much for you. My life, the whole world, they're yours, if only you'll take them. Will you, *alma mia?*"

She looked as if something was tearing her apart. Before he could blurt out his demand that she reveal whatever burden she had for him to bear, she surged into his body. "Yes, please, please, Durante. I want to never be without you again. I want to live my whole life enriching yours, if only you'll let me."

He groaned as if his soul had been dragged out and suddenly left to return to its sanctuary deep within him. He crushed her in his arms, moaned the ache of relief. "You have already enriched it beyond imagining, *mia cuore.* You healed me, purged my anguish. Now I owe you, us, myself without bitterness or shadows anywhere inside me. I owe you the best man I can be. And you were right, as you always are. This can only happen if I let go of my anger. I also need to give you the wedding that you deserve, and all of that can only happen one way. By going back. To make whatever peace I can with my father, to marry you on Castaldinian soil."

Thirteen

With every mile deeper into Castaldinian soil, it rose.

The suffocating feeling of being dragged into the worst days of her life, of feeling that they would start again, and this time, they would never end.

Gabrielle had spent what she remembered of her childhood on a Mediterranean island. Although that childhood had been turbulent, the sheer beauty and brightness of the backdrop it had played against had ameliorated much of its anxieties and heartaches. That had been reversed during her last stay in Cagliari.

Witnessing her mother fade away in that sun-drenched, olive grove-ensconced villa, watching her eyes empty of life on that veranda overlooking her beloved white-gold beaches and azure bay, burying her in the embrace of the land she'd called home, had forever linked this magnificence of nature, this balminess of weather, with irretrievable loss and bottomless grief.

Now similar scenes unfolded before her eyes, the influence of another ancient, blessed-by-the-gods land permeating her senses.

She took what comfort she could in the differences she'd been discovering since they'd started their drive to the capital, Jawara, from the private airfield Durante's jet had landed in.

Castaldini's landscape was wilder, more varied, segueing from mountain chains with rivers traversing them to plains with lakes and ponds that softened the harshness of the craggy terrain they rolled from. Then, at the very edge of the island, the land gave way to dense maquis followed by miles-deep expanses of powdered gold lapped by what seemed to be liquid turquoise.

Durante embraced her, as if feeling her turmoil. "This is your first trip here, isn't it, *bellissima?*"

Tell him. Tell him now.

The urge almost burst her heart. It had been doing so ever since he'd asked her to marry him two days ago.

Dread had won out then. It won out again now. Weakness, too. She'd snatched at his offer without coming clean, and she still couldn't do that now. And in an hour's time they'd meet the man who could reveal the secret he'd made her keep. She dreaded Durante's reaction, but at least she'd finally breathe easy that it was out.

For now she was powerless to do anything but let him clasp her to him. "It is strange that I never came here."

Stranger than she could let on, with her lifelong relationship to King Benedetto.

"But it was your connections to this land that led you to find me. And this convinces me. Someone out there must really want to reward me. I wonder what I ever did to deserve that much? I must have done something huge. Why else did I find you? Why else do you love me? But even if I didn't deserve you before, I'll do everything I can, for the rest of my days, to deserve the gift of you."

Awe and gratitude deluged her. She clung harder, until she felt as if she were submerged in his flesh, his love. "Don't start me on correcting you about who's the gift here." After an endless moment of supercharged communion, he looked away as if compelled, watched the scenes going by. "You miss it. It's been five years?"

"Months," he muttered. "I came back after *Padre's* stroke."

"But you said…"

"I couldn't stay away. I stayed until he was out of danger. Paolo and Clarissa have been supplying me with constant reports of his condition ever since. But I swore them to secrecy. Needing to make sure he is all right has nothing to do with forgiving him, as *they* both seem to have done."

"But you're willing to give him a chance now."

He seemed to struggle for an answer. He had pledged it to her, but it was tearing him up. King Benedetto had better have something solid to put Durante's mind to rest, or she would be the first one to tell Durante that the king didn't deserve his turmoil.

She stroked his hair until he moaned his enjoyment. "Don't say anything, *amore mio*. Whatever happens, I just want you to be at peace."

"I am, now that I have you. And I want you to be at peace, too. Remember when I told you not to worry about… anything?"

She nodded slowly. She'd almost forgotten. She'd been pulling her company back into the black just by working to full capacity the past three weeks. The news of Durante's book was also restoring stockholders' faith with a vengeance.

"The moment I realized that the recession in Castaldini wasn't temporary, I started making plans to put an end to it. I slowed down their implementation when Leandro came into the picture, giving me time to perfect them instead of rushing in without every long-term outcome accounted for. Then I met you, and I felt I owed it to our love to consider nothing else but us for those short weeks. Now everything is in place, so you have nothing to worry about, but my plans have to wait a bit longer while I give you a wedding and a honeymoon like no bride has ever had."

She turned in his arms. "But the simplest wedding is all I want, and every day with you is like a hundred honeymoons. Don't you worry about my company. You've done way more than enough and we're going to be fine. It's Castaldini that needs you now, and I can't have you putting off any work because of me or I would have failed in my most basic function as your lover and wife—to give you the peace of mind that will make you even more productive and effective."

He let out a shuddering sigh. "It's hopeless. I'll never find words or deeds enough to express how much I love you." Suddenly his lips crooked. "Now have mercy and let me give you what I need to give you without exhausting me. I need all my stamina for all that work ahead of me."

She melted into him, deluged by another wave of love and wonder. "I called it right the first time I saw you. *Sietto un uomo cattivo.*"

Jawara was very much what its Moorish name said it was. A jewel of a city, glittering bright and unique under the perfect heat and illumination of the Mediterranean sun. It nestled between the banks of a river, which Durante informed her was the Boriana, and an imposing, vegetation-covered mountain, the Montalbo. The rolling plains to its north and south looked like a carpet.

Durante had warned her that the past decade had taken its toll on the city's former flawlessness. But Gabrielle couldn't see the deterioration that he as a native discerned. The place looked pretty incredible to her. She'd been to almost every European and North African capital in the last few years, and Jawara was the only one that didn't have one building younger than the seventeen hundreds. It looked like an ancient city transplanted into the twenty-first century, a mixture of Gothic, Moorish and Baroque architecture and influences that she'd never imagined could mingle in homogeneity, but that here was simply breathtaking.

As they came to the first cobblestone street, the royal palace came into view, crouching like a gigantic, ancient creature on a hill that dominated the oldest part of the city.

On entering the palace grounds, a complex of enormous buildings surrounding the central palace, Durante pointed out the National Library, the Royal Museum, the ceremony halls and government offices. He said it would take some time to get to the Royal Apartments, because they were at the end of ten miles of grounds and he wasn't asking Giancarlo to drive faster over the cobblestones and risk giving her a headache. When they drove past the central palace itself, she gaped, comparing it to a twilight zone episode in which someone passed a never-ending building. Durante laughed, said it was just another of his family's pretentiously sized places. It did lie over four-hundred-thousand square feet.

Then the car stopped. In seconds she was smiling up at Durante as he opened her door even as her heart stampeded.

In a few minutes they'd see King Benedetto. And her horrible burden would be lifted. And then…?

"If it isn't the prodigal prince returning."

The deep drawl had Durante relinquishing his smile and turning on his heel. She followed his gaze and did a triple take.

Strolling toward them was a man who, while looking nothing like Durante in features or coloring, made almost his same impact, in size and height and in sheer radiation of power and charisma. It took her a moment to realize who he was. Prince Leandro D'Agostino, the one-time rebel, once-exiled prince, now regent of Castaldini.

"Leandro! My regent!" Durante exclaimed as he strode toward him with open arms.

Durante pulled his cousin into a rough embrace, one Leandro reciprocated, adding thumps on his back before drawing back to grin widely. "You're looking absolutely radiant."

Durante guffawed. "I thought the term was reserved for

brides. Preferably our brides." He looked back at her, elation turning his beauty from breathtaking to heartbreaking, before he looked at the woman Gabrielle noticed coming up behind Leandro with tranquil steps. He turned to Leandro with a quirked eyebrow. "But then, *you're* absolutely glowing."

"Indeed, I am. Any wonder with such a power source?" Leandro put his arm around the woman's shoulders, gathered her to him in a gesture so eloquent with tenderness, possessiveness and dependence that it sent a frisson of emotion through Gabrielle, at how much it mirrored what Durante blessed her with. The woman—who must be Phoebe Alexander, the sister of Durante's sister-in-law and Leandro's brand-new bride—smoldered reciprocation into her husband's adoring eyes.

Phoebe was the first truly silver-eyed person Gabrielle had ever seen. She was gorgeous, with all that glossy black hair and creamy skin. She looked blissful. And pregnant. The fact that she was showing meant she'd been already pregnant before the wedding.

Something hot and overwhelming stormed through Gabrielle, lodging into her womb. She'd never thought of having a baby. Until Durante. How she yearned to have his. She prayed to God she could.

"So miracles do happen." Phoebe was looking at her in candid and benign interest. "I never thought the day would come when anyone softened the inflexible Durante."

Gabrielle took her hand, grinned conspiringly at her. "So you're a power source, and I'm some sort of softener. We must put our disparate abilities together in an unstoppable collaboration."

Leandro sighed, winking at Durante. "We're doomed."

Durante looked heavenward. "From your lips."

They all laughed as they started walking into the palace, the men falling into step with each other, as she did with Phoebe.

The conversation flowed with bantering ease, to her immense relief. Phoebe was going to be a constant presence in her life and it would have been a source of unneeded strife if they hadn't hit it off. But she felt they'd only like each other better on deepening exposure. It felt so good, looking forward to this unexpected bonus. A woman her age, in her same unusual situation, becoming an ally, a friend. Something she sorely needed.

Suddenly they both fell silent. It seemed Phoebe's ears had pricked like hers on hearing the turn in conversation their men had taken.

"He isn't in good shape, Durante. Take it easy on him."

"I *am* taking it easy on him. I came back, didn't I?"

"Not enough, *amico mio*. Give him a chance. Let him talk this time. Maybe he has something to say."

"If he did, he would have said it years ago."

"You already tried thinking the worst and it ate up five years of both of your lives. Why not try giving other possibilities a chance? I would have thought you incapable of relenting on this one, but because you are here, I am hopeful that miracles indeed do happen."

After a moment's silence, Durante turned, caught her eyes in a searing look of passion and tenderness and whispered, "They do."

Gabrielle almost cried out with the slam of emotion.

And she prayed. For this miracle of his love to overpower whatever ugliness there was, even if there was no hope of erasing it. To overlook the unwilling deceit she'd perpetrated.

"Durante. You came back."

Durante looked at the man who'd once been his hero. The father he'd idolized. He almost didn't recognize him.

Pain seared his heart. He refused to give in to it. "*Sì.* But not for you. For Gabrielle."

He held out his hand to her. Her gaze was frozen on his father's face as she unsteadily came to his side. "Gabrielle Williamson, my bride-to-be. We're getting married here in a week's time. It's for love of her, for needing to give her a future untainted by the shadows of the past that I'm here, *Padre*. But I've also met you halfway. Now it's your turn. Tell me the truth."

"The only truth, Durante..." His father's weakened voice revved sickness and regret behind his sternum. He gritted down on the weakness. "...is that there was no villain or victim."

"So you didn't have a mistress?"

"No, I did have a mistress." Gabrielle lurched at his side. He barely stopped himself from exhibiting his own shock at having all his doubts validated. "And she was the only woman I ever loved. She was the one, Durante. Like your Gabrielle is to you."

The lava of betrayal and hatred and anger rose in him, obliterating all his intentions to give peace a chance. "And of course you discovered this after you married a woman who gave you her heart and life and children."

"I loved that woman before I ever met your mother. I banished her over insane and wrong suspicions and married your mother on the rebound."

Every word was prodding skewers deeper into his wounds. "So not only was my mother your victim, but the other woman, too."

"Your mother was my queen. But I was not in love with her. Neither was she with me. She married me to become queen. I thought she was what the crown needed. When I renewed my relationship with the woman I loved, I kept it a secret for many reasons, your mother's feelings not being among them. She wouldn't have cared."

"Why did she write all that, then? If she wasn't going literally insane with jealousy over your loving another?"

His father seemed to shrivel back into his bed. "I...I don't know. But there's nothing to be gained from digging up skeletons."

Accumulated heartache and confusion and disappointment erupted through him like a geyser. He lunged forward, wanting to shake his father and roar for him to put him out of his misery. He was hiding things. Things that would make every-thing make sense.

Then he felt it. Gabrielle's hand trembling on his arm.

He cursed himself. He'd sworn he'd never distress her again, and here he was, forcing her to witness him resurrecting his family tragedy.

He pulled her into him, looked his entreaty for forgiveness into her reddened, teary eyes, his heart compressing at having caused her such anguish.

Then he turned and almost wept himself at seeing the dev-astation on the face of a man he'd thought indomitable. He had to believe at that moment that his father might also prove to be not as heartless as Durante believed him to be.

"We'll leave skeletons in the past, *Padre*, even if they come out of the closet sooner or later. Now, the future and all I am belong to Gabrielle."

As he supported the almost-collapsing Gabrielle and turned to lead her out, his father's thick, tear-filled rasp stopped him. *"Gabrielle."*

Gabrielle lurched in his hold as if she'd been shot. Durante almost had to support her full weight as he turned them around.

His father was smiling, a smile distorted by the devastation his stroke had left in its wake. It twisted Durante's heart. And that was before his father rasped, "Thank you for bringing my son home...*figlia mia.*"

Fourteen

The wedding was tomorrow.

And Gabrielle was going insane.

King Benedetto had pretended he didn't know her. She'd been so shocked that she'd gone mute.

Then Durante had taken her to his apartments, drowned her in his passion until she'd forgotten that a world outside him existed. Before she could remember, he'd swept her into the whirlwind of preparations and one chance to tell him after another slipped by.

She needed to see King Benedetto before she could reveal the truth to Durante. This was the first day he'd been allowed visitors since they'd seen him. His health had taken a turn for the worse after his confrontation with Durante.

She waited until the king's valet had left them alone before she blurted out her agitation and fear. "Why didn't you tell Durante of our relationship? It's been killing me, keeping my word, but I believed you finally would. He might...*would* have understood then, that it was never my intention or idea to hide facts from him. Now, after that stunt you pulled, I'm dreading the worst."

The king struggled to sit up in bed, reached a trembling hand to her. "No, Gaby. He loves you so much he'd give his life for you. He wouldn't blame you for abiding by the promise I made you give me. But I can't tell him of our relationship and neither can you."

"But this is ridiculous. It's bound to come out sooner or later, and then what would you have me say? Oops, I forgot to tell you, your father was my family's benefactor?"

"It's imperative that Durante never find out."

"Why?" she cried out in confusion.

The king seemed to age another twenty years before her eyes. Then he finally slumped back in bed and whispered, "Because if he finds out, he'll put two and two together and realize that my mistress, the only woman I ever loved, was your mother."

The world receded, her vision narrowed. Cold flooded in on her from all sides. Her heart lost momentum, stuttered, stalled.

The king's voice became distorted. "I wanted to take our secret to my grave as she did. We never wanted you of all people to find out. But I have to tell you now."

She felt her heart bleeding. "Not true…Mom loved Dad…"

"She did, but it was nothing like the love she had for me or I for her. She met him in my court, married him years after I left her in heartache and misery. It was almost as soon as she had you that your father's depression began to manifest. Then I found proof that my suspicions—which had led me to break both of our hearts—had been unfounded. I sought her out, begged her forgiveness for the way I'd treated her. When I offered them my support, it felt as if your father suddenly let go with me around to carry the burden. She'd suffered so much,

I had to offer her solace and then it was beyond us not to succumb to our love. Your father wasn't there by then, either mentally or emotionally, to notice let alone care.

"We kept our relationship a secret so that we wouldn't hurt our children, but we were deeply in love and perfectly happy. Then she started to suffer from her rheumatoid arthritis and I started to let go of my own life and duties as I suffered her suffering. She chose to die without me around to witness it. Getting the news of her death, knowing that I wasn't there for her in her last days, was almost a deathblow. I held on until I attended her funeral, made sure that everything was in order with her legacy and with you before I broke down. The only reason I'm still hanging on now is, I need to hand over Castaldini to a new king.

"I always wished Durante would be that king. But the laws were against it. Then he came to despise me so much he wouldn't have accepted becoming my crown prince even if the laws changed. Then everything changed after your mother died, after I almost did. After Leandro turned down the crown, I had my chance to finally change the laws, to make Durante eligible despite his being my son. But the hard part was getting Durante himself back here. That's when it finally came to me—the one thing that could bring him back, to me, to himself. *You*."

"How did you *know* that?" she wailed. "God...*why me?*"

"Because, although I risked exposing everything by bringing you together, I had to try to give you what I and your mother could have had if I hadn't spoiled it for us. I sent you to him because you're so like your mother and he's so like me, I was certain you'd fall as madly in love as we had. And you did."

Durante stared down at the report in his hand.

He'd been trying to put the past into its inaccessible corner, never to touch the present or future again.

He hadn't expected to end his own world.

His knees gave way under the enormity of the conspiracy the cold data spun.

"Durante!"

Durante heard the booming voice, the powerful footsteps' escalating tempo as if through a separate consciousness. It felt as if it were another's body that was dragged to its feet, that stumbled backward to hit something soft and yielding that broke its falling momentum.

"Durante, what's wrong?"

He stared up out of eyes that felt alien, at a stranger with concern and anxiety blazing on his face. Somewhere in the black cascade that eclipsed everything, he knew this was Leandro, his cousin. But was he really? Did he know who anybody was anymore? Hadn't it all turned into one big, convoluted lie?

"Did something happen? Is Gabrielle all right? The king?"

"Something happened. Gabrielle. The king." Durante heard the stifled echo droning in a monstrous parody of his voice.

"What *is* it, Durante? *Tell* me."

Durante wanted to tell him. He felt sure that uttering the words would finish him. And he wanted it all to be over. But his mind and tongue had lost their connection.

Leandro sat down slowly, as if afraid any sudden movement would make him crumble. He pried free something Durante was crushing in his fist. The report. The end of his world.

Every nerve in his body snapped. He fell back like a skyscraper coming apart in an earthquake.

Numbness crept over him like an army of spiders as Leandro looked at the papers. Nothingness expanded in his skull until he thought he felt the lines connecting its bones separate, widen, as if in preparation for explosion.

He pushed back against the inexorable pressure. "Read it. Out loud. From the beginning."

Leandro gave a grudging nod and began to read.

"Investigations reveal that when King Benedetto was newly crowned, he had a secret lover, Clarisse LeFevre, a French-Canadian ballerina in an Italian ballet company that frequently performed in Castaldini. He broke off the affair over reports that she was cheating on him with a business rival, and almost immediately married Countess Angelica Boccanegra. Ten years later, the king, after investigating and proving the falseness of the allegations that had caused him to cast away his lover, finally located her. She was now married, but he became a constant presence in her family's life, supporting them all after her husband, Andrew Williamson, suffered bankruptcy and depression. He had them all relocated to Cagliari, where he also kept a private home, where it was revealed after intensive investigation that he met with her regularly and in utmost secrecy a few months before her death seven months ago."

"And a month later he had his stroke." Durante heard the whisper, didn't recognize it as his voice. "He weathered my mother's death without a tear, but almost died when his lover did. The lover he named his own daughter after. The daughter of the woman he was betraying, the woman he broke in mind and spirit. And that lover's daughter is now my bride-to-be. The love of my life."

Leandro fixed him with a blank stare. Durante knew his lightning-swift mind was calculating all possible outcomes of every comment he could make.

Leandro finally exhaled. "I admit, this is totally unexpected. I can imagine how shocked you feel."

"Can you, Leandro?" Tendrils of fury began to rise among the ashes of deadness. "Can you imagine what it feels like to surrender your heart only to find out you've fallen for your enemy?"

Leandro's jaw hardened. "That is shock talking, Durante. Gabrielle has nothing to do with your parents' affair."

And the fury ignited. "*She lied.* She pretended she didn't know my father—*Dio,* she blinded me so completely I never suspected a thing. And all the time she's been lying…about *everything*."

"Don't start jumping to conclusions," Leandro said, like a father chastising sense into an overemotional son. "There could be a perfectly good reason why she couldn't reveal their connection."

"There *is* a perfectly good reason. Gabrielle's reputation includes a warning not to let her within a mile of you. She knew I would never have met with her had I known. She played me so seamlessly, she had me groveling for believing the rumors about her instead. *Dio!* The hurt she poured out, the act I bought to the last tremulous treacherous gasp. I trusted her so much I didn't even *think* of investigating her. And she's been deceiving me all along. She's—"

"Durante, *stop*." Leandro's growl was like a pressure bandage slammed on the hemorrhage of his rage and agony. "I once jumped to conclusions, listened to my fears and prejudices about Phoebe, and I ended up wasting eight years of our lives. Eight endless, miserable years of our living apart and in emotional exile. Don't make the same mistake. The price is incalculable."

And the torrent of pain gushed again. "Did Phoebe turn out to be the daughter of the woman your mother died of a broken mind and heart over? Did she keep lying to you until she had you depending on her for your every breath so that you wouldn't be able to break free once you learned the truth? Is she a cold-blooded, manipulative cheat?"

Leandro's gaze hardened to flint around the core of burning empathy. "All I can say is that this is circumstantial evidence, and I've learned the hardest way possible how misleading that can be. But as impossible as it may be for you to think right now, there are more important things at stake than your heart. Castaldini is in danger. The financial dangers are the least of our problems and the easiest to deal with. Political and ethnic conflicts are brewing, and as regent I don't have the influence of a king. Everyone believes they can wait for my proxy to be over—they don't feel the necessity to bow to my power. Castaldini needs a king."

"What does that have to do with this?"

"It has everything to do with it. The king has forbidden anyone to reveal to you his intention to approach you with his demand before he judged the time right to do so himself, but I believe none of us can afford to wait anymore. I can see that your personal situation is about to blow to kingdom come, and you *cannot* let that interfere with your decision."

"What decision? What the devil are you talking about?"

Leandro looked as if he were about to stab him, hating to do it but knowing there was no escape. "After I declined to become crown prince, the king had the Council make an exigency amendment to the laws of succession. By this new amendment, he can now make you his crown prince. If you agree." Leandro took him by the shoulders, shook him. "As you should, Durante. As you *must*."

And it all made sense. Sick, macabre sense.

His father had set out to *make* him agree.

He'd known nothing would bring Durante back—nothing except an irresistible woman armed with thorough knowledge of him so she could project the image of his soulmate.

And she'd manipulated him to the point where they would achieve their objectives. At his expense. His father would get back the son who'd rejected him, would pass the crown to his line through Durante, while Gabrielle, the king's partner in crime, the daughter of the woman he'd loved above all else, would be that son's worshipped wife and queen, as his father had failed to make her mother.

His father was going to make his demand today. He knew it. And if he'd still been blind and fathoms-deep in love and trust, he would have agreed to anything to keep peace and harmony.

He exploded to his feet, rage and agony boiling his blood.

Leandro shot up, caught him. "Don't do anything in this state, or you'll regret it for the rest of your life."

"*What* life?" Durante roared as he pushed his cousin away with all the violence tearing apart his insides before staggering away, a mortally wounded beast bent on slashing apart the two people who'd killed him before he surrendered to oblivion.

Gabrielle stared at herself in the bathroom mirror, whimpered as she brought the ice cube again to her swollen eyelids, trying to ameliorate the swelling.

She'd been back in her quarters for an hour now. She'd run there to get a hold of herself, but she'd failed miserably.

Shock and misery still wracked her. It felt as if acid were gushing through the gaping cracks of her shattered world.

How *could* they? Her mother, and King Benedetto? All these years, lying to her, to everyone?

Now everything made sense. Why her mother had always had that look of apology, why she'd sent her to a boarding school in Napoli when she was old enough to suspect what was going on.

Betrayal ate at her. But it was nothing compared to the dread that tore at the tethers of her mind. If she felt this way, what would Durante feel when he found out?

The king had said he should never find out. But this couldn't be hidden. Not anymore. And she had to be the one to tell Durante the terrible truth.

She had to do it now. Before their meeting with the king. Come what may. Even if it was something she might not survive.

The icy feeling had reduced the telltale signs of weeping, but she still looked like she had on the day she'd lost her mother. She felt as if she had lost her all over again. She might lose her life now. She would, if she lost Durante.

No. No, she wouldn't. Durante believed in her now. He'd know she had nothing to do with any of it. He trusted her.

She staggered out of her suite…and was almost knocked off her feet by the wall that materialized in her doorway.

Durante! God…here…no, she needed a few more minutes…

Stop it. This had gone on long enough. It ended now.

"Durante…I need to tell you something."

"What a coincidence. I have something to tell you, too."

His voice. She'd never heard his voice like that. Emotionless. Lifeless. He looked as if he'd been crying, too, his eyes shards of brilliant blue simmering in angry redness.

She clutched at him, her heart bucking its tethers. "Durante, what is it? God…are you okay?"

"I will be."

Then he turned and walked away. She rushed in his wake, a fireball of fear and confusion exploding in her mind.

The king was waiting for them at his reading table, the first time she'd seen him out of bed. His face started to tug into that skewed smile. It fell back into bleakness at the sight of Durante.

Silence settled over the scene. Something terrible radiated from Durante. She stumbled sideways as if out of the path of a lethal ray.

He couldn't already know. She had to be the one to tell him.

But he looked…rabid. He…he *did* know. Was incensed. But not at her. It couldn't be at her.

"You wish me to become your crown prince." The hiss that emanated from him sounded inhuman. Shudders started to creep over her. "What do they say about being careful what you wish for? You manipulated me to get me back here only for me to find out your secrets, crimes that I will expose. I'll tell the world what a sadistic, adulterous husband you were. And I will take the crown now, not after you die."

Gabrielle's heart had stopped with the first salvo out of Durante's lips. Now it beat like the wings of a hummingbird, yet pushed no blood to her brain. The world constricted into a pinpoint of darkness.

Something wrenched her from the edge of oblivion. Durante was dragging her away.

He was so angry at his father. She had to defuse his shock and agony. Had to mend this horrific breach.

"Durante...don't do this to yourself...it's not like you think..." His abrupt stop had her crashing into him. She leaned on him, for support, for both of them, her lips trembling into his heaving back, with love, with desperation to explain before one more minute passed. "Your father's only crime was loving my mother, hiding their affair, from everyone, starting with me, but he did it so that he wouldn't hurt anyone...he loves you...but was so afraid you hated him, made me promise..."

He wrenched away, turned on her. "You were congratulating yourself, weren't you? As each phase of your seduction worked on me like a spell?"

Seduction? Spell? What did he...?

"Now you've reached the point where you believe your hold on me is unbreakable, that I'd sooner let go of all my pride and fortune, of my very life, than let you go, don't you?"

He-he believed...the worst? *Again?* He didn't trust her? Didn't think she deserved a chance to defend herself?

"And you were right."

Wha...? She'd misunderstood? He wasn't saying that he doubted her?

"I would give my life for you, the woman, the treasure who shares my soul and mind, the owner of my body and heart."

He wasn't! He didn't doubt her. Her churning world stilled, quaked with relief. "Oh, God, Durante, oh, my love..."

"But that's not you." His hiss froze her jubilation. "That woman was a role you played to seduce me, reading the lines my father taught you. That woman doesn't exist. So now, my bride-to-be—you're no longer my bride-to-be. I cancelled the wedding. I'll tell the whole world why. I'll show anyone who had any doubt about you how the worst so-called rumors were only the tip of the iceberg. I'm cancelling the book deal, too, and if you try to play any of the penalty clauses, I'll crush you and your precious company under my foot." He gave a hideous laugh. "Oh, wait, I'll crush you and everything you hold dear, anyway."

A stranger. She was looking at a vicious stranger. One who'd played an elaborate game of make-believe, of knowing her down to her last thought, caring for her with his every breath, respecting and trusting her with his every fiber. It had all been empty. All the proclamations, the promises of forever.

The world started spinning again, swinging her away with it. He receded as everything drowned in a sea of distorted images.

"Gabrielle."

That growl, a predator enraged to find his prey about to escape his talons. She turned back, no survival instinct left.

And he delivered the killing blow. "If you have any shred of self-preservation left, you will make sure I never see you again."

She stared into his cruel eyes, and everything came to an end.

Fifteen

Leandro had been right.

He'd warned him. Durante hadn't listened. He'd been deaf. Blind. And totally out of his mind.

Madmen didn't realize the depth of their insanity. Didn't see it at all. Saw it as justified action, inescapable reaction.

He'd foamed and fermented in the delusion, thrashed and plummeted down a spiral of intensifying agony. Then he'd hit bottom. And he'd remembered them. Gabrielle's eyes. In the blood-red haze of his fevered memories. The shock of letdown there, the horror of loss. The realization that the one who'd pledged to protect her from all harm, the only one she'd trusted with her true self, was the one dealing the deathblow. And he'd known.

She had nothing to do with any of this. Hadn't known most of it. What she'd hidden had been the burden, the pain he'd seen in her eyes. That she couldn't tell him what wasn't hers to tell. She'd tried to tell him that.

He believed her. Without question. Now. When it was too late.

No. He couldn't let it be. He wouldn't. He would do anything to turn back the clock. Erase the hurt he'd inflicted on her.

But he'd resurfaced from his madness to find her gone. Two days ago. He'd learned that she'd left within an hour of his throwing her out of his life with a threat he wouldn't have hurled at his worst enemy. But he'd thought her far worse than that then. He'd thought her his murderer. When he'd been the one who'd stuck a knife in her heart. And twisted.

He didn't deserve her forgiveness.

But he would. Whatever and however long it took, he would.

Gabrielle counted her steps, her breaths. The seconds.

It was the one way she could go on from one to the next. She had this conviction that if she stopped counting, she'd stop moving, stop breathing. Stop moving forward in time. Be trapped forever in a second of pure agony.

She wished she would. But couldn't. Not before she made sure her employees were safe from Durante's wrath.

She cared nothing for what he would do to her.

She opened her office door, stepped inside, the plush wall-to-wall carpeting absorbing the sound of her steps, amplifying the feeling that she'd ceased to exist.

But it wasn't insubstantiality that engulfed her now. It was something else. Something overwhelming and all-encompassing.

Him. Durante. *Here.*

She dropped the count. She'd been right. Her breath stopped. Time. The second held her in its grasp—and crushed her.

"Gabrielle. Perdonami."

Forgive him?

The second fractured. Breath tore into her lungs. She spun around. And there he stood.

A god come down to earth, in an immaculate suit the color of the night of his hair, he made the crisp blues and grays of her space—made *existence*—pale into colorless nothingness.

His scent, his eyes on her. They made her forget everything. Every muscle in her body quivered like a bound bird's, the blinding urge to fly to him tearing her apart.

Weak, self-destructive moron. She might never truly live again, but it was his doing. He'd crushed her.

What more did he want?

Anguish almost ripped her chest open. "You didn't cut me into small enough pieces to satisfy your self-righteous rage? You want to see me a bloody mass on the ground before you're satisfied?"

"Gabrielle, *no.*"

His urgency exploded into strides that obliterated what remained of the flimsy safety of distance, brought him against her, around her, hard and hungry. Then he was taking of her, taking her into him again, spreading her against him, pressing her between the persistence of his passion and something as unyielding, drinking in her moans, absorbing her shudders, draining her of will and memory and pain.

He was the air that would make her breathe again. But he was also the poison that would asphyxiate her if she did.

She tore herself away, stumbled against the wall at her back, pressed against its coolness. "So is this it? You…invested too much time and effort in…training me, and even though you despise and abhor me, you want your sex-marathon-on-demand nympho back?"

"No, Gabrielle, don't… Don't say anything like that."

"You mean you *don't* want to have sex with me? That wasn't why you almost took me against the wall just now?"

"No, Gabrielle—yes, I desire you, now and always, but that isn't why I'm here. I now know the truth, and…"

She cut him off. "So you deigned to talk to your father? Oh, wait, you think his word is as worthless as mine. So you must have done more investigations. And they…what? Cleared me? No, thanks. I'm not doing this again. I'm guilty of not telling you how it all started, when it wasn't my secret. But you accused me of *crimes*. You found such comfort in believing the worst without even trying to hear me out."

He neared her as if approaching a wounded, terrified animal, his voice a hypnotic croon. "I was in shock, in agony, over finding out you're the daughter of the woman I spent years hating without knowing if she even existed. I went mad thinking you knew all along and had been leading me on. But I didn't need you to slap sense into me this time, Gabrielle. What we shared, what I feel for you, what I *know* you feel for me, made me overcome the pain and madness. I did no investigations. And I didn't talk to my father." Hesitation entered his beseeching eyes. "What would he have told me?"

His words swirled inside her brain, making no sense. She refused to let them. They'd be lethal if they did. She'd succumb to their influence. Sink. All the way this time. And next time he gutted her and tossed her out to drown, she wouldn't resurface.

But among all the things she couldn't hear, there was one thing she could. A question. About his father.

She owed him no answers. Not after he'd judged and executed her. But he wasn't just the man she'd loved beyond self-preservation, would love against all reason, for the rest of her days. He wasn't just the one being who held the power of destruction over her, who'd used it again and, she swore, for the last time. He was also the man who held the fate of a kingdom— and that of his father—in his hands. She knew her mother would have wanted her to do anything she could to defend the one man Clarisse LeFevre had lived and died loving. Gabrielle's answer might exonerate King Benedetto in his all-powerful son's eyes. Or at least ameliorate his guilt. Durante might not exact his revenge on his father to the full.

She told him everything she knew.

Durante listened to Gabrielle, his heart twisting in his chest. She seemed sentient but not alive, aware but unfeeling, held together with the glue of automations and obligations, which was bound to come undone at any point. Even if it didn't, and it stuck her together, fractures traversed her psyche and soul, fault lines that would splinter her again at the least pressure.

He'd done that to her. And he had to restore her, at any price. Starting with his own life.

He'd hoped that begging her forgiveness would garner him a hearing. Why had he hoped she'd grant him what he'd denied her?

He knew why. He'd counted on her being more forgiving than he was. But even her mercy had limits. He'd pushed her beyond them.

One hope remained. That something in what she'd said would give him insight into how to repair the devastation he'd wreaked.

He replayed every word, looking for clues. He got only blows, every one battering him with more shame at how he'd lashed out at the two people who'd put their pride and hearts on the line to save him from his bitter loneliness, to help him find contentment and joy, to learn what living truly meant at last. The one thing to redeem him was that his heart had already believed in her without proof, against all damning evidence.

It *had* all been his father's orchestration, as he'd thought when he'd been in the throes of suspicion and pain-induced insanity. But not at all as he'd expected. His father did know him far better than he knew himself. He knew Gabrielle as deeply. He'd known it would take Gabrielle to save him, bring back his humanity, that it would take *him* to heal, cherish and worship her. So his father had sent her to him.

And though it had started out as a mission for her, their magic had taken over from their first glance, fulfilling his father's prophecy.

But it had been the king's fault again that she'd kept secrets. He'd made her pledge secrecy, fearing the violence of his son's unreasonableness, the depth of his bitterness, things that would have made him blind himself to her true worth, costing him the one woman who shared his soul. Even when it had seemed that nothing could tear them apart, his father had still withheld the truth, fearing exactly what Durante had done upon finding it out.

Another verdict was as glaring. He might never know the true causes of his mother's decline and death, but whatever those diaries contained, something else must have caused her to write them. His father was no cold-blooded abuser. Thinking otherwise had poisoned him for five long years. But the heart that had led him to loving Gabrielle would never lie to him. His father, while guilty of many things, had never been guilty of hurting his mother.

He not only owed Gabrielle a lifetime of apologies, he owed his father, too.

"...but instead of exonerating your father," Gabrielle was going on, "I must have only added manipulating us to his offenses, in your opinion. Or rather, manipulating you, because I've been in on it, with the worst possible agenda, of course. So why not get on with your revenge? End your father's reign in humiliation, take the crown from him, take my company from me, throw me out on the street and leave me the hell alone."

"That was my rage talking," he insisted, urgency writhing in his chest. "I would never have carried out my threats."

"Really? So cancelling the wedding, telling the world why—"

"I told no one anything. And far from taking your company away, I'm here to give you these." He flicked open his briefcase, handed her a dossier. When she didn't take it, he explained. "These papers ensure that neither I nor anyone else can take your company away, that it will always be stable no matter what happens to any market in the world. And that's just the beginning. Make any demands. I'll do anything for you. *Anything,* Gabrielle. My father knew me, and you, too well— he knew we were made for each other. He did what he had to do, to bring us together, a debt I can never repay."

"So you won't dethrone him?"

"I was raving mad with shock when I said that. The moment I came to my senses, there was no question in my mind about your innocence."

"Sure. Until the next time something rouses your suspicions, and you turn on me and maul me to death."

"That is never going to happen again."

"I've heard that before, Durante. From Ed. Every time he abused me, he'd say it would never happen again."

"I'm *nothing* like him. Don't, *Dio,* please don't…don't put me in the same thought as him, *amore.*"

"You're worse than him." Her sob sliced into his brain, its agony, its import, insupportable. "I cared nothing for him. His abuse cut nowhere beyond the surface. Yours carved me to the marrow."

Her agony flooded his chest, became molten lead coursing through his left arm like the onset of a heart attack. He wished it would truly damage him. But self-abuse was self-indulgent. He needed to be at his fittest to undo what he'd done.

He wrestled with paralysis, surged forward to embrace her. She struggled like a cornered animal. He was distressing her more.

He staggered back, rasped, "I followed in my father's footsteps—this genetic compulsion we once spoke about—to the point that I suspected the worst of you, the keeper of my soul, and cast you away, as he'd done with your mother. But he let her stay away, compounded his mistake by marrying for the crown, and made a mess of so many lives. But I'm done being my father's son. I'm walking my own path from now on and I'm repeating no one's mistakes, starting with my own. Give me one last chance, Gabrielle. I'll never ask for anything more. I'll make amends, until the end of my days."

Tears no longer flowed from her eyes. She was no longer shaking as if she'd unravel, no longer breathing as if her throat were swelling closed.

Dared he hope...?

"Words are cheap, Durante." Her voice was steady, lifeless. "To you, everything is cheap. You can throw companies and fortunes at me, but the one thing I want is what you've failed twice to give me. The benefit of the doubt. Fair treatment. I once said, when you were as generous with superlatives, that 'never' has forever scope. I *should* have waited and seen.

"I thought at the beginning that I could handle it, if you were offering something simple and superficial, like no-strings sex. But you weren't, and even though I told you I wasn't in your league, I let you sweep me away, into all those powerful emotions and bottomless passions, let you seduce me into wanting—and expecting—too much, way too soon. I was right to be wary of your rash proposal, and again too weak to heed my wariness. I own my mistakes—whether it was falling into your arms then believing we could have forever, or abiding by a promise of secrecy, not only because I couldn't break my word, but because I feared for the fool's gold perfection of what I thought I had with you.

"Whatever you feel for me, it's not enough to overcome everything it has against it. You might think now that it's 'until the end of your days,' but give yourself, say, a month or two. *And* a woman or two. I bet you'll forget about me. Or maybe, when all the illusions have dissipated and nothing but desire remains, you'll walk back into my life like your father walked back into my mother's and be my part-time lover, too. If you're still single, that is. Whatever happens, the dream, the grand and unique and indestructible love, the guaranteed forever, is over. You ended it. And from where I'm standing, it's better this way."

He had no idea how he remained on his feet.

He'd thought he'd known how much he'd hurt her. Until she'd hurt him back. Caused him irreparable damage just by giving him a good look at her wound. He knew now. He also understood. Why his father had lost so much of himself when his lover had been suffering, why he'd almost died when she had.

He had broken her trust. Not just in his ability to always treat her with restraint and respect, but in the depth and constancy of not only his feelings but his character. More pledges now would mean nothing. Worse than nothing. His amends had to be undeniable, until she believed him and in him again.

And if she couldn't? If this was irreversible?

He laid the dossier on her desk, leaned burning palms and trained blind-with-tears eyes on it. He couldn't consider this. Not if he wanted to remain alive to see his plan through.

"Non rinuncerò mai ad amarti. Sono tuo per sempre."

I will never give up loving you. I'm yours forever.

His only indication that the words that had scraped their longing into his mind had actually left his lips was the lurch that shook her, the two wet trails that spilled down her haunted face. He filled his soul and senses with one last look at her, a sight that would fuel him during the desolation of being without her. Then he turned and walked away.

It felt as if he was walking away from life. As he was.

Sixteen

The door clicked closed. Durante. Gone.

She'd made him go.

Something skewered its way through her gut. An unvoiced scream. For him to come back. That she took back every word. About not trusting him. Not forgiving him. Not believing in his love. Not feeling as if she'd die if he forgot her, if he sought out others, if he sought her out again with nothing but lust in his heart and body. *She'd lied.*

But she'd had to.

She couldn't have let him prove to her how much he loved her. How much he regretted doubting and hurting her. For she would have believed again, surrendered all the way now that her last shackle—his father's secrets and her fear of their exposure—had been lifted.

But Durante's shackles would never be lifted. Not when they were created by her very identity. The daughter of the woman he believed had caused his mother's devastation and death. That knowledge would poison his love, would chip away at its foundations. Then his bitterness and paranoia would rise again and he'd decimate her, forever this time, under the brunt of his cruelty.

She crumpled to the ground.

She'd gotten home, somehow. She didn't remember how. She'd found herself there, weeping. She hadn't stopped since. It was morning now. She thought.

Her nerves flamed with impulses, her mind roiled with obsessions, her cells burned with longing.

She needed him back.

How could he not come back? Was that it? The extent of his all-powerful emotions? His unstoppable persistence? She'd slapped him with words, clearly trembling for a repudiation, and he'd taken them as cause to give up on her? He was really gone?

He *couldn't* be. He'd said he'd never give up. Why had he? Wasn't what they'd shared worth more than an hour's cajoling and a few pledges? Had all feeling been on her side, after all?

Which would make sense. More than a man like him feeling the same absolute emotions for her as she did for him.

But he'd said he *did.* And he never lied.

So had he faced himself with the truth, that in time he'd wonder how he'd disregarded who she was? Was he now wondering just how much of their rapport was real and how much had been his father's tutoring? Could suspicion be taking hold of his mind again?

If it was, then his mind was a time bomb and she shouldn't even think of coming within a mile of him again. She couldn't survive another blow up.

But…she could have carried on in her lifelessness if he hadn't shown up yesterday. How dared he jump-start her heart and hopes, then walk away again? This time she wasn't flatlining, as she had the first time. This time she was fibrillating, the spikes of chaos intensifying by the second, threatening to rupture her heart…

Stop. You're not doing this. You're not following in your father's footsteps. Or his mother's.

She had to behave as if she was alive, go through the motions. In time, it was bound to simulate life, maybe even re-spark it. She had to go through her morning routines, take them, and the rest of her life, one second at a time.

She dragged herself out of bed. One foot in front of the other. A shower, breakfast, morning show on TV, dress, work. Wait for him, pray for him to contact her again. She'd take him back if he did, grab at anything he offered, offer all of herself again come what may…

No, no, *no*. If she wasn't right for him, it would end far worse than any of their parents' stories had ended. For she was sure none had loved this intensely.

She walked back to the living room, taking a sip of her orange juice only to inhale one then spew it out in a fit of coughing.

His voice.

God, she was starting early, imagining hearing it.

Her eyes panned to where she thought she'd heard it issuing from, and she almost choked on her lungs in shock. He was… he was…

On TV. On the morning show she watched every day.

The gawking, swooning, hyper-excited female anchor was squeaking, "So why did you decide to break your silence with the press, Prince Durante? And in this spectacular way, too?"

Durante turned his brooding eyes from the woman's face to look directly at the camera. Gabrielle collapsed under the brunt of his stare. She knew every woman in the globe would be similarly affected, but she knew. He was looking at her.

Then he began to speak, dark, driven, unraveling her with each syllable and intonation. "I am here offering the love of my life a public apology, issuing a plea that she give me one last chance. I am announcing that Gabrielle Williamson's Le Roi Enterprises—besides publishing my biography, which will include the details of the situation that led to my…postponement of our wedding—will also have the exclusive on every public plea I'll continue to issue. Also, as a token of my total love and absolute trust, I have signed over all my holdings to her."

Among the bombs, she realized one more thing.

This was on air live. Right in front of her building.

She'd never thought anything solid could move so fast. She streaked out of her apartment, saw that the elevator was in use. She didn't even think of waiting, ran to the stairs and down the ten-floors, a missile set on Durante.

Once outside her building, she barreled her way through the barricade of human flesh he towered above. The crowd parted each time someone recognized her, and murmurs and exclamations spread like wildfire in dry tinder.

Her momentum slammed her into him. He barely moved under the impact. Hesitation, something she'd never felt from him, filled the arms that steadied her. His eyes devoured her as his face clenched with such longing, regret and entreaty that her chest heaved from their bombardment far more than with exertion.

His lips worked for a moment before they started to open. She just knew he was going to say more crazy, compromising things.

Her hand lurched up, clamped over his mouth. "This is all a publicity stunt, world," she panted. "A dare I didn't dream he'd take me up on. So…stockholders, don't panic. And tabloids, don't hold your breath. He will *not* be revealing anything, as there's nothing to reveal. And yes, the book is going to be great, and everyone should preorder their copy, but it will not contain any sensational confessions, just the secrets to this…this phenomenal powerhouse of a dreamboat's success, okay? What's more—"

"Non posso più vivere senza di te, Gabriella mia."

Her voice vanished, every electrical impulse powering her body shut down. She sagged in his arms. He was singing. Here.

I can't live without you, my Gabrielle.

The crowd gaped. All of New York City seemed to hold its breath. He continued the song he'd written for her, had proposed with, his voice setting the yearning lyrics on passionate fire, turning the evocative melody into all-encompassing enchantment.

A hush reigned after his last vibrato had died away.

Then a storm of applause and questions exploded.

"Did you write this song?"

"Will you be recording this song?"

"Will you release it as a single? Part of an album?"

He shrugged. "It's Gabrielle's song. She decides what I do with it." He turned his eyes down to her, his all-out surrender stoking the inferno raging inside her. "Just say the word and I'll turn it into a rock number and perform it in a jumpsuit—"

She surged up, sealed his lips with hers, shutting him up.

He sagged in her arms, groaned his relief long and shuddering into her mouth, shaking the foundations of her soul. Then he suddenly dropped down. She panicked. For a millisecond.

He wasn't fainting. He was bending for leverage. Then she was in his arms, feeling weightless, his gaze, the emanations of his whole being making her feel priceless.

The sea of bystanders parted, raged with hoots and applause. She vaguely thought New Yorkers must be reveling in the unfolding of yet another chapter in the fairy tale of their resident Castaldinian prince and his commoner American princess.

She missed the journey back up to her apartment. She only knew she was on her bed, her world once again anchored by Durante's beloved weight, the heat and hardness of his steel-fleshed body driving security and equilibrium back into hers.

A long time after the frenzy unleashed in the wake of the barely escaped catastrophe abated, she lay boneless and throbbing with satiation, cleaved into him, sighing her bliss. "That was quite a stunt you pulled down there."

Durante pressed into her, almost entering her again "down there," purred, "Glad you approve."

She wanted nothing more than to have him inside her again. But this couldn't be put off. She dug her nails in his buttocks, stopping his movement.

He groaned in disappointment, rose over her, his eyes growing serious. "It wasn't a stunt. I was showing you everything I held dear, my privacy, my pride, my status, my achievements, are a negligible price for regaining your trust. None of them mean a thing without you."

Her heart swelled until it seemed to fill her down to her toes. Seemed it squeezed against her now ever-filled tear glands. "I won't let you do any of the things you said you'd do."

"I already did them.

"You're undoing them, right this second."

"I can't. It's all yours now."

"Okay, Durante, this long ceased to be thrilling and is getting pretty scary. Stop. Now! Before this crazy stunt backlashes, you crazy, insane man."

"I was insane to hurt you. I've never been saner or clearer about what matters. You, the restoration of your pride, your trust in me and my love. All I need is for you to let me be yours…yes, until the end of my days." His lips crooked. "I just hope you'll let me give you advice on what to do with your newly acquired wealth, so your stockholders don't suffer a cent's devaluation in the transfer. That's the only catch, really, that you can't give it all away to your favorite charities and causes."

"But I can give it to anyone I want, right? So I'm giving it to you. End of conversation." Something enormous mushroomed in his eyes, until she almost wailed. "What now?"

"I was just wondering. Who else would toss back something of that magnitude, without even pausing to make me sweat it first? Not that I am sweating it. I don't care about it at all. I made my billions, and I'll just make more. In fact, on the way here, I made a transaction that resulted in half a billion in my newly emptied account. I'm not destitute, if that what you're worried about."

"I'm not worried. I'm *disintegrating*."

"While I'm rejoicing. If I managed to prove the extent of my trust. Even though you're making it so hard to prove anything by tossing everything back to me like that, I hope you know I wouldn't have risked anything with such catastrophic potential to so many if I didn't trust you more than I trust myself."

"Everything has to be larger-than-Jupiter with you, doesn't it? I toss around a few stupid words when I'm upset, and instead of giving me those couple of days—of hours you once suggested—to get my act together, you fling a whole financial empire at me."

"And my kingdom, for good measure." He sighed in contentment.

Suspicion sank its ice into her bones. She exploded out of his arms, sprung standing on the bed. "God, what did you *do*?"

He spread his magnificence like a replete lion, hooked his hands behind his head. "I told my father to go for his third candidate for the crown."

Her heart almost fired out of her ribs. "What do you think I am? An insane goddess appeased only with atrocious sacrifices?"

"You are my goddess, but you're regretfully too benevolent. You tried to stop my sacrifices, are trying to reverse them now."

He stirred, prowled on all fours to her, bent to kiss her feet. She cried out the surplus of emotion. He crooned worship, worked his way up her legs, her calves, the back of her knees, burning one fuse after another, congealing the valves of her heart. She collapsed at the first touch of his tongue inside the thighs that trembled again with the need to wrap around him.

He received her nerveless mass in his cherishing arms, cosseted all of her quivering flesh. "This has nothing to do with what happened between us. But it is the best course of action *for* us. We're both too much citizens of the world, too invested in our careers. As much as I love Castaldini and know you can come to love it, too, I don't see our life bound to it."

She squirmed. "God, no, don't even consider my career in this decision. I'll find a dozen ways to maintain it. I'm sure you can work out as many ways to run your empire by remote control. Take this back, *please*."

"I won't, because it's the right thing to do. If I'm crowned, it will pulverize the law that made Castaldini such a unique and prosperous kingdom until my father's personal life interfered with his being the formidable king he was. My reign would be the end of the crown for merit. And I truly think King Antonio had a great idea in making the king work for his crown, not be born to it."

"But the law is too absolute and unfair," she protested. "Many sons won't live up to their fathers' level, but you've surpassed yours. It would be glaringly obvious you were made king on total merit, that after you the law would be enforced again, until another king's son proves himself as worthy of the crown."

"Even if I'm worthy of it, I didn't grow up dreaming of it, wasn't fighting for it when I built my success and fortune."

"But that should only make you even more worthy of it!"

"It doesn't work that way in Castaldini. And then, I truly don't *want* the power and the responsibility, and that's a *huge* strike against me. All I want is to be yours."

There were no limits to the heights he'd make her scale.

She pitched herself from those heights into the depths of arms she knew would always be there to catch her. "It's too much!" He rumbled. She swallowed his protest, sobbed. "Don't contradict me. I'm stating facts here."

He chuckled. "Here's one more fact, *bellissima*. My father, too, believes the long-term repercussions of the precedent of my crowning would change the face of Castaldini, something we should all fight against. He was desperate for me to take the crown, not because I was Castaldini's last hope, but because he feared the Council's rigidity. They proved it by choosing me over the third candidate because he's an illegitimate D'Agostino, a factor that in this day and age shouldn't be a consideration. He still fears they'll let him, the one they know would probably make the best king go because of this stupid prejudice."

She raised an eyebrow, suspicion and hackles rising. "Going overboard alert. Losing all credibility here. Way to go to *de*-convince me. There can be no better king-material than you."

Delight crackled from his depths, rich and infectious and unbearably arousing. "Never stop saying things like that to me."

"No danger of that whatsoever. Just hope you can stomach all the nonstop adulation. So what's this exaggeration about this third candidate making the best king?"

"It's what I believe. We—my father's candidates—are on par as far as power and success go. But I believe Ferruccio is the one among us who has that most drive to lead. He's also the most… old-fashioned, if you will. And he might never admit it, but he craves setting down roots, which he's never had. That combination makes him the best choice for Castaldini's king. I pray they make him the offer and fast, and that he agrees to take up the mantle when they do. I'm not sure he will. If I were him, I'd probably courier the D'Agostino family and Castaldini to hell."

"What if he does refuse? Will you then take the crown?"

"I won't think of that unless I'm the last candidate left standing. But I agreed to be Leandro's co-regent. Once Ferruccio is crown prince, we'll be his main men on his new Council, continuing to do our utmost in Castaldini's service. That means many, many visits there. Would you like that?"

She plunged into his embrace, kissing him all over. "I would love that! And I love you, most of the time beyond endurance…"

She cursed herself for the tremor in her voice when he

heaved up, his eyes alert, alarmed. "What is it? Surrender all your worries, *anima mia,* let me erase them."

"I-I'm just so afraid…and that was the reason I…"

"The reason you said what you did yesterday."

"I always forget that you can read my mind."

"Just partially now. I can't tell what still pains you so."

"I-I…oh, hell…tell me the truth, okay? I'll know if you don't and it will prey on my mind. You *really* don't care who I am?"

"I couldn't care more." She jerked, and he gentled her, leaned her against his propped up thighs, stroked and kneaded her, at once mind-blowingly sexual and heart-meltingly emotional. "You are the one who has awakened my heart, reawakened my ability to care, to enjoy, introduced me to the full potential of life. You have nothing to do with our parents' choices. I was insane to suspect you of knowing of their affair, to doubt your motives toward me. But at the core of my madness was my fear that I didn't deserve you and all the happiness you bring me, that something would happen to prove it was all too incredible to be true."

"And even though you deserve to be punished, slowly, agonizingly…" She lunged at him, kissed her way down his body until he growled, thrust at her, drove convulsing fingers in her hair to stop her, to urge her on. "…you also deserve far more than I can possibly be or give…hush, don't contradict me again." She raised her eyes, found that his were rivaling Castaldini's shores in vividness and translucency, radiating pure azure adoration. "And that's the same fear that paralyzed me into keeping silent. I couldn't believe this could be happening to me. I was living in dread of ending the perfection."

His lips quirked. "So you don't think it was fool's gold?"

She fluttered her lashes. "So you don't think I seduced you?"

"You did seduce me. To the point that my mind unravels at the merest thought of losing you." Distress gurgled in her throat. A slash of bedeviling white lit up his dark gold face as he hauled her to him. "And *Grazie a Dio* that you did. You seduced me just by being yourself, with no motive other than being unable to have enough of me. But *ragazzaccia mia,* you stopped my amends too soon. Not that I'll stop. I'll just keep on making them, keep showing you, proving to you what you are to me, my everything."

"Them's fightin' words, Your Highness. Prepare to witness that you are this and more to me. For starters, I'll never withhold anything from you again, not facts, not the last shred of thought or emotion." She bit her tongue. "Uh…that sounded as if I'll be a blabbering, overemotional pain in the rear."

"This kind of pain?" He squeezed her buttocks, pressed her into his aroused flesh, groaned as if in suffering. Her insides clenched, needing, gnawing. She knew how he felt. "Or the other kind, where you agonize me by reassuring me I'm in your heart and thoughts, that I'm pleasing and pleasuring you? If that's the kind of torment you have in store for me, I beg you to never stop."

She opened herself to him, pledged with body and soul, to never, ever stop.

Much, much later, she was draped over her man, her lover, the most incredible gift in this plane of existence, feeling savagely pleasured and overcharged with satiation.

It was why the thought, when it came, ripped through her like a hot knife through butter.

He felt it at once, gathered her more securely. "Tell me."

She didn't hesitate this time. "You still don't know what really went on with your mother, what her diary meant."

"I know she was disturbed. From the thankfully little I saw of my grandfather, I can see why, now that I've opened my mind to other possibilities rather than the obvious ones pointing to my father."

"So you don't believe your father drove her to suicide?"

He shook his head. "Or your mother. It was a tragedy, but I believe my father now, that there was no villain."

"Do you *really* believe that, or are you just—"

"Manipulating history to get closure in a way that would exonerate both our parents for obvious self-serving purposes?"

"Will you quit finishing my thoughts and questions?" She scraped her teeth against the abrasion of his stubble.

He groaned his pleasure before he pulled back, his eyes solemn. "And no, I'm not deluding myself here. I punished myself and my father long enough for the failures I believed we were both guilty of. But finding you gave me the clarity to see that neither of us could have done anything to help her, just like neither you nor your mother could help your father. I also faced it that neither of us could have suspected Clarissa's ordeal, that we did intervene immediately when we found out. I was never able to forgive either of us for this. But loving you opened up my ability to forgive, to let only positive emotions thrive."

The serenity he exuded enveloped her, the freedom from darkness that blazed in his eyes lighting up the universe. Searing joy spilled from her eyes, as for the first time she knew the real meaning of security, of stability. This was unshakable.

He suddenly frowned. "*Dio mio,* what a fool I am!"

She jerked up. "What?"

"I dared presume you'll walk down the aisle on the strength of a proposal I effectively rescinded."

"It's okay. It's reusable. Like a 'get out of jail free' card."

He guffawed as he jumped up, scooped her up in his arms. "If you ran a jail, I'd never want to get out. Now, will you lend me your yacht? I want to reenact a certain proposal scene."

"Oh, God! You still haven't taken all your stuff back."

"You make it sound like some old clothes and a guitar."

"Just tell me how to get everything back in your name or I'll hold my breath until I pass out!"

He sighed, let her down on her feet. "I trust this won't be the way you operate with me from now on?"

She gulped a breath and he shook his head, grudgingly walked away, reached down to his strewn clothes for his cell phone.

He'd hit two numbers when she cried out. "Wait!" He cocked a daunting eyebrow at her. "You're penniless right now, right? Comparatively speaking?"

"*Sì.*" His eyes flared and subsided like blue pulsars as he prowled back to her, running his hands suggestively down his chiseled body. "Why? Do you have a…position for me?"

She glowed up at him. "Many, permanent ones. In my bed. And everywhere else."

"Hmm. Do I get to be…on top sometimes still?"

"On top, under, behind, around. All positions are…wide open."

"I can say I'm interested." He licked his lips. "Rabidly so."

She hauled him to her in a ribs-cracking hug. "You just want me for my money." She giggled and sobbed and deluged him with kisses. "So, Your Scrumptiousness—now that I've proven, from my exalted upper-hand position, that I want you for you, will want only you, will love, cherish and defend you, be there for you with all that I am, for the rest of my days, *sposami,* Durante. Marry me, *amore mio.* Make me complete."

He hugged her off the ground, the elation and adoration radiating from him enough to power the whole city with years of love and wonder. "On one condition. If I say yes now, I still get to do my reenactment."

"Say yes now and you can do whatever you like, always. In fact, you'd better."

"You'll let me give you all that I am?"

"Oh, yes, please."

He let her down, kneeled, still hugging her, his eyes pledging more than his all. "Then, yes, *amore mio.* Love me and let me love you…forever."

She hugged him into her, body and being, bliss shaking her, gushing from her eyes. And she knew.

There'd never be doubt again.

This *was* unshakable. This was forever.

* * * * *

Another D'Agostino prince has found his soulmate,
but the crown and kingdom are still at risk.
Don't miss the stunning conclusion
to THE CASTALDINI CROWN,
THE ILLEGITIMATE KING.
On sale July 2009.
Only from Olivia Gates and Silhouette Desire!

*Celebrate 60 years of pure reading pleasure
with Harlequin®!*

*Harlequin Presents® is proud to introduce its
gripping new miniseries,*
THE ROYAL HOUSE OF KAREDES.
*An exquisite coronation diamond, split as a symbol of a
warring royal family's feud, is missing! But whoever reunites
the diamond halves will rule all....*

*Welcome to eight brand-new titles that unfold to reveal the
stories of kings and queens, princes and princesses torn
apart by pride and power, but finally reunited by love.*

Step into the world of Karedes with
BILLIONAIRE PRINCE, PREGNANT MISTRESS
Available July 2009 from Harlequin Presents®.

ALEXANDROS KAREDES, SNOW DUSTING the shoulders of his leather jacket and glittering like jewels in his dark hair, stood at the door. Maria felt the blood drain from her head.

"Good evening, Ms. Santos."

His voice was as she remembered it. Deep. Husky. Perfect English, but with the faintest hint of a Greek accent. And cold, as cold as it had been that awful morning she would never forget, when he'd accused her of horrible things, called her terrible names....

"Aren't you going to ask me in?"

She fought for composure. Last time they'd faced each other, they'd been on his turf. Now they were on hers. She was in command here, and that meant everything.

"There's a sign on the door downstairs," she said, her tone every bit as frigid as his. "It says, 'No soliciting or vagrants.'"

His lips drew back in a wolfish grin. "Very amusing."

"What do you want, Prince Alexandros?"

A tight smile eased across his mouth and it killed her that even now, knowing he was a vicious, arrogant man, she couldn't help but notice what a handsome mouth it was. Chiseled. Generous. Beautiful, like the rest of him, which made him living proof that beauty could, indeed, be only skin deep.

"Such formality, Maria. You were hardly so proper the last time we were together."

She knew his choice of words was deliberate. She felt her face heat; she couldn't help that but she damned well didn't have to let him lure her into a verbal sparring match.

"I'll ask you once more, Your Highness. What do you want?"

"Ask me in and I'll tell you."

"I have no intention of asking you in. Tell me why you're here or don't. It's your choice, just as it will be my choice to shut the door in your face."

He laughed. It infuriated her but she could hardly blame him. He was tall—six two, six three—and though he stood with one shoulder leaning against the door frame, hands tucked casually into the pockets of the jacket, his pose was deceptive. He was strong, with the leanly muscled body of a well-trained athlete.

She remembered his body with painful clarity. The feel of him under her hands. The power of him moving over her. The taste of him on her tongue.

Suddenly, he straightened, his laughter gone. "I have not come this distance to stand in your doorway," he said coldly, "and I am not going to leave until I am ready to do so. I suggest you stand aside and stop behaving like a petulant child."

A petulant child? Was that what he thought? This man who had spent hours making love to her and had then accused her of—of trading her body for profit?

Except it had not been love, it had been sex. And the sooner she got rid of him, the better.

She let go of the doorknob and stepped aside. "You have five minutes."

He strolled past her, bringing cold air and the scent of the night with him. She swung toward him, arms folded. He reached past her, pushed the door closed, then folded his arms, too. She wanted to open the door again but she'd be damned if she was going to get into a who's-in-charge-here argument with him. She was in charge, and he would surely see a tussle over the ground rules as a sign of weakness.

Instead, she looked past him at the big clock above her work table.

"Ten seconds gone," she said briskly. "You're wasting time, Your Highness."

"What I have to say will take longer than five minutes."

"Then you'll just have to learn to economize. More than five minutes, I'll call the police."

Instantly, his hand was wrapped around her wrist. He tugged her toward him, his dark-chocolate eyes almost black with anger.

"You do that and I'll tell every tabloid shark I can contact about how Maria Santos tried to buy a five-hundred-thousand-dollar commission by seducing a prince." He smiled thinly. "They'll lap it up."

* * * * *

What will it take for this billionaire prince to realize
he's falling in love with his mistress…?
Look for
BILLIONAIRE PRINCE, PREGNANT MISTRESS
by Sandra Marton
Available July 2009 from Harlequin Presents®.

We'll be spotlighting a different series every month throughout 2009 to celebrate our 60th anniversary.

Look for Harlequin® Presents in July!

THE ROYAL HOUSE of KAREDES

TWO CROWNS, TWO ISLANDS, ONE LEGACY
A royal family, torn apart by pride and its lust for power, reunited by purity and passion

Step into the world of Karedes
beginning this July with

BILLIONAIRE PRINCE, PREGNANT MISTRESS
by
Sandra Marton

Eight volumes to collect and treasure!

REQUEST YOUR FREE BOOKS!

2 FREE NOVELS PLUS 2 FREE GIFTS!

Silhouette Desire®

Passionate, Powerful, Provocative!

YES! Please send me 2 FREE Silhouette Desire® novels and my 2 FREE gifts (gifts are worth about $10). After receiving them, if I don't wish to receive any more books, I can return the shipping statement marked "cancel". If I don't cancel, I will receive 6 brand-new novels every month and be billed just $4.05 per book in the U.S. or $4.74 per book in Canada. That's a savings of almost 15% off the cover price! It's quite a bargain! Shipping and handling is just 50¢ per book.* I understand that accepting the 2 free books and gifts places me under no obligation to buy anything. I can always return a shipment and cancel at any time. Even if I never buy another book, the two free books and gifts are mine to keep forever.

225 SDN EYMS   326 SDN EYM4

Name	(PLEASE PRINT)
Address	Apt. #
City	State/Prov.	Zip/Postal Code

Signature (if under 18, a parent or guardian must sign)

Mail to the **Silhouette Reader Service:**
IN U.S.A.: P.O. Box 1867, Buffalo, NY 14240-1867
IN CANADA: P.O. Box 609, Fort Erie, Ontario L2A 5X3

Not valid to current subscribers of Silhouette Desire books.

Want to try two free books from another line?
Call 1-800-873-8635 or visit www.morefreebooks.com.

* Terms and prices subject to change without notice. Prices do not include applicable taxes. Sales tax applicable in N.Y. Canadian residents will be charged applicable provincial taxes and GST. Offer not valid in Quebec. This offer is limited to one order per household. All orders subject to approval. Credit or debit balances in a customer's account(s) may be offset by any other outstanding balance owed by or to the customer. Please allow 4 to 6 weeks for delivery. Offer available while quantities last.

Your Privacy: Silhouette Books is committed to protecting your privacy. Our Privacy Policy is available online at www.eHarlequin.com or upon request from the Reader Service. From time to time we make our lists of customers available to reputable third parties who may have a product or service of interest to you. If you would prefer we not share your name and address, please check here. ☐

SDES09R

Silhouette *Desire*

COMING NEXT MONTH
Available July 14, 2009

#1951 ROYAL SEDUCER—Michelle Celmer
Man of the Month
The prince thought his bride-to-be knew their marriage was only a diplomatic arrangement. But their passion in the bedroom tells a different story….

#1952 TAMING THE TEXAS TYCOON—
Katherine Garbera
Texas Cattleman's Club: Maverick County Millionaires
Seducing his secretary wasn't part of the plan—yet now he'll never be satisfied with just one night.

#1953 INHERITED: ONE CHILD—Day Leclaire
Billionaires and Babies
Forced to marry to keep his niece, this billionaire finds the perfect solution in his very attractive nanny…until a secret she's harboring threatens to destroy everything.

#1954 THE ILLEGITIMATE KING—Olivia Gates
The Castaldini Crown
This potential heir will only take the crown on one condition—he'll take the king's daughter with it!

#1955 MAGNATE'S MAKE-BELIEVE MISTRESS—
Bronwyn Jameson
Secretly determined to expose his housekeeper's lies, he makes her his mistress to keep her close. But little does he know that he has the wrong sister!

#1956 HAVING THE BILLIONAIRE'S BABY—
Sandra Hyatt
After one hot night with his sister's enemy, he's stunned when she reveals she's carrying his baby!